# Dolphinea

## Quest for the Tidal Heart

A
Novel

## Daniel Wheeler

First Edition

ISBN 13: 978-0-9853284-2-9

Front Cover Artwork: © justdd - Fotolia.com
Back Cover Design: © Lulu Templates. Lulu.com
Photo and Graphics: © Daniel Wheeler
Author: Daniel Wheeler
Self Publisher: Daniel Wheeler
Published in the United States of America

First Printing: Lulu.com
Print is last number listed:
10  9  8  7  6  5  4  3  2  1

Disclaimer: This book is a work of fiction. All names, similarities to actual persons, creatures, places, incidents, or historical events, are the product of the author's imagination or used fictitiously. The author makes no claims to the authenticity or accuracy of any such similarities or material used, and any resemblance to real events, persons, or creatures, living or dead, is entirely coincidental.

# ໑ BEGINNINGS ໑

Genesis 1:20-22 And God said; "Let the waters bring forth abundantly the moving creature that hath life, and fowl that may fly above the earth in the open firmament of heaven." And God created great whales, and every living creature that moveth, which the waters brought forth abundantly, after their kind, and every winged fowl after his kind: and God saw that it was good. And God blessed them, saying, "Be fruitful, and multiply, and fill the waters in the seas, and let fowl multiply in the earth." ~ Bible Scripture (King James Version)

Throughout history, myths and legends about dolphins, whales, and porpoises have been shared. Humans have always had a unique and close relationship with these sea creatures, which remains unchanged even after thousands of years. Aristotle once wrote that dolphins are not afraid of humans and often approach ships at sea to play and frolic around them, even when sailing at full speed. It is possible that Aristotle could only observe what was happening on the ocean's surface and could only imagine the strange and mysterious world beneath the waves.

My name is Dolphinea. I am a young adult male Atlantic Bottle-nose Dolphin descended from a long line of dolphin cetaceans of the family Delphinidae. I live in the warm, tropical ocean areas of the Florida Keys and the waters of the Caribbean Sea. I also enjoy swimming in shallow inland temperate waterways and tributaries. My mother gave birth to me in February and kept me by her side until I was around 4 or 5 years old. Our bond is unbreakable. I was raised with my brothers and sisters in a community known as a pod.

As a member of a pod of dolphins that includes my relatives and other dolphin families, one of our primary functions as a pod is to provide a safe environment for social learning and building relationships. Within our pod, we engage in activities such as playing, learning, alerting each other to external dangers like predators, practicing courtship, and hunting together. We also travel as a group, which allows us to hunt, gather food, and stay protected. Even though I am an individual, I still like to explore independently. However, I understand there is safety in numbers, so I always return to my pod. Occasionally, I mingle with other pods, making new friends outside my group.

Our pod has an incredibly complex social structure with a strict hierarchy that dictates everything from feeding to mating. At the top of the hierarchy is our pod leader, a position held by the oldest and most experienced dolphin in our group. Our leader oversees all significant decisions, including where to go and when to take a break.

Underneath our leader are a few senior dolphins who act as advisers and help enforce our leader's decisions. Most of the dolphins in our pod are middle-ranked, primarily focusing on daily activities such as food foraging. The junior dolphins are at the bottom of our pod hierarchy, typically younger and less experienced than their counterparts. While junior dolphins may not have much say in pod decisions, they play an essential role in keeping the group together and helping to care for calves.

Since I am a young adult, I fall into the middle-ranked group. My primary responsibilities are to forage for food, keep alert, and inform the other pod members of dangers and predators. I also teach our younger members how to hunt in groups, how to vocalize, how to use their navigational skills, and how to develop their ability to cooperate with other group members to survive and thrive. That doesn't mean I have no time for play, making mischief, or forming alliances with other males around my age in our pod. Our alliances will last a lifetime and are formed for two primary reasons: females and fighting.

Our male friendships are very complex and similar to those of a human male group. We create partnerships for cooperative purposes. Our coalition helps us monopolize females, increasing our access to females for mating opportunities.

Additionally, having an alliance increases the chances of success during aggressive encounters with the much larger bottlenose dolphins, sharks, other predators, and, of course, the dolphin bullies, who occasionally need to be taught a lesson or two!

I am known by my male companions for my adventurous and curious nature, often exploring the vast ocean depths to discover new creatures and environments. I am a skilled hunter, using my echolocation to locate schools of fish and then working with my pod to corral them into tight groups. I am also a talented singer, using a series of clicks and whistles to communicate with other dolphins and express my emotions.

I consider myself a social creature and enjoy spending my time with my family and friends. I am fiercely loyal to my pod, and I will do anything to protect them from danger. In my free time, I enjoy playing games with my fellow dolphins, leaping out of the water, and performing acrobatic stunts. My favorite foods are shrimp and crabs, squid, and small fish like herring, cod, or mackerel. Despite the many challenges that I face in the wild, I remain optimistic and resilient. I try to be an inspiration to all who know me and a testament to the strength and beauty of my heritage and lineage.

# ❧ CHAPTER ONE ❧

In the vibrant depths of the Caribbean ocean, Dolphinea glided gracefully through the crystal-clear waters. His sleek, silver-blue skin shimmered in the dappled sunlight that filtered through the waves. With each powerful stroke of his tail, he propelled himself through the liquid expanse, leaving a trail of sparkling bubbles in his wake. Dolphinea's eyes sparkled with curiosity and a deep understanding of the ocean's mysteries, reflecting the wisdom that came from generations of dolphin heritage.

As he descended into the ocean's embrace, the coral beds and marine life below acknowledged his presence with a shimmering display of colors. He dove into the mysterious realms beneath the waves, exploring hidden caves and ancient coral gardens that whispered tales of the sea's enigmatic history.

With a powerful flick of his tail, Dolphinea propelled himself toward the surface, breaking through the ocean's boundary with a spectacular burst of water. Sunlight cascaded through the splashes, creating a sparkling crown around him. His dorsal fin emerged first, followed by his glistening body as it arched gracefully into the open air. A symphony of droplets danced around him, catching the sunlight like liquid diamonds. The playful exhale that followed echoed across the ocean, a melodic celebration of the seamless dance between "Dolphinea" and the ever-changing tides of his watery kingdom. As he took a deep breath, he let out a series of clicks and whistles and exclaimed, "I love being alive and free!" With another deep breath, he plunged back into the depths, feeling every wave caress his body and every current and ripple remind him of how lucky he was to be a creature of the sea. He realized that being unrestrained and alive meant endless possibilities.

Dolphinea's eyes were filled with joy and excitement as he leaped out of the ocean, expressing his love for freedom. He gracefully breached the surface of the water after a deep dive, and his sleek body broke through the glistening waves. His curious eyes scanned the horizon, and he spotted a distant boat sailing on the open sea. Intrigued, he began to swim towards the boat with a blend of fascination and caution. With a rhythmic dance beneath the water's surface, he approached the boat, marveling at this human-made vessel that intruded upon his watery realm. The distant silhouette became a focal point for his boundless curiosity.

As I approach the sailboat, I am reminded of what my parents would always tell me. They used to say that encounters between dolphins and sailors at sea often created positive and memorable experiences for the sailors. For dolphins, it's more about harnessing the energy generated by the boat's movement through the water. However, they also warned me to be extra careful when approaching sea-going vessels. I like to bow-ride. I like riding the bow waves created by boats. I enjoy gliding along the side of the boat and in front of the bow. Leaping and twisting in front of the boat or darting through the water alongside a sailing vessel brings me joy and a sense of connecting the world of humans to my natural world. I have been told that sailors often describe a sense of camaraderie with dolphins during these interactions, as if we, as dolphins, are welcoming them to our maritime domain.

I want to share something with you. While watching us dolphins can be an enjoyable experience, boat operators need to approach us with care and respect. Boat traffic, particularly in popular marine areas, can threaten us and other marine life due to collisions, noise pollution, and disturbances of our natural environment and behaviors. I have witnessed and heard stories about injuries to other dolphins caused by misjudgment (getting too close to the bow or props) and negligent actions by boat operators that caused injury. Unfortunately, not all boat operators and sailors are responsible humans. Some do not understand the need for care and respect for other creatures, especially at sea. That is why I must stay alert and maintain a safe distance from the bow, particularly from the stern of powered boats with propellers. I have to be aware of my speed and position at all times. Encounters with boats and humans during bow-riding add a sense of adventure and wonderment to life at sea, creating cherished memories.

My uncle Jinn would tell me stories about dolphins and fishermen. Uncle Jinn is not a blood relative and was not born initially into our pod. He is an Asian dolphin, not an Atlantic bottle-nose. He says he is an Indo-Pacific Humpback Dolphin and regularly reminds everyone that he is from a rare dolphin species that lives only in coastal waters around China and Taiwan. How he arrived in the Caribbean and the Atlantic is anybody's guess since the stories about his life vary depending on his telling and retelling. But he has been welcomed into our pod as family. He has a loving nature with some rough edges. With a sleek, silver-gray body adorned with subtle hues of pink and white, he exudes an ethereal beauty. He is knowledgeable, with a knowing wisdom. When he speaks, you listen. No doubt because of his many worldly adventures and the ancient wisdom he has picked up along the way. Uncle Jinn is also known for his distinctive sonar calls, which are almost magical, resonating with a soothing melody that captivates all who hear them.

According to the lore surrounding Uncle Jinn, he is said to have been born in a hidden underwater cave, where the energies of the ocean granted him special abilities. It is believed that he can communicate not only with other dolphins but also with various sea creatures and even some mystical beings that dwell in the depths. Rumors abound that Uncle Jinn has the ability to navigate through underwater portals that lead to other realms, making him a mysterious and revered figure among both marine life and those who explore the oceans. Many sailors and adventurers seek out tales of Uncle Jinn, hoping to catch a glimpse of the wise dolphin that holds the secrets of the deep.

Uncle Jinn has taught me many things. He told me that fishermen and dolphins often share a complex relationship shaped by the proximity of their habitats and their interactions in the marine environment. On one hand, fishermen may view us dolphins as both companions and competitors in their pursuit of fish. Of course, we are known to be highly intelligent individuals who have developed sophisticated hunting techniques. Sometimes we take the opportunity to capitalize on the efforts of fishermen by gathering in the wake of their fishing boats to catch disoriented or fleeing fish. This association, while beneficial for us dolphins, can be a source of frustration for fishermen who may perceive us as depleting their catch or interfering with their operations. They have not realized that we are only taking the fish that have fallen from their nets.

On the other hand, fishermen and dolphins have occasionally formed unique partnerships. In some parts of the world, particularly in traditional small-scale fisheries, we have been known to work together with fishermen in a mutually beneficial manner. I mentioned before that we are very good hunters. We can herd schools of fish toward waiting fishermen, making it easier for them to catch their prey. This cooperative dynamic reflects the complex and nuanced interactions that occur between us and the fisherman's human activities. Some, but not all, fishermen are aware of this intricate balance between competition and cooperation in our shared marine ecosystem.

As I got closer to the sailboat, I could see its white sails billowing in the ocean breeze, and I couldn't resist the urge to leap gracefully out of the water. As I leaped high above the water's surface, I noticed a pod of dolphins also approaching the vessel. I could tell by their clicks and whistles that they were not my family pod. They were another, different pod. I could hear the distant echolocation clicks and joyful chirps of this pod echoing through the vast expanse, drawing me towards the gathering. As I approached, the anticipation in the air was palpable, and the excitement radiated from the pod as they sensed my arrival. I could see that the pod was a tight-knit community of dolphins.

As I approached, they responded with synchronized clicks and whistles. They formed a welcoming circle, their bodies dancing in the water like liquid poetry. I was filled with enthusiasm, joining in with the pod's joyful chorus as we communicated in a language that transcended words. The exchange of sonar signals and playful flips bound us together. As we expressed our mutual desire to do some bow-riding and general dolphin play, we arrived at the boat. Approaching the vessel on both sides, our dorsal fins broke through the surface in a synchronized dance. We bow-rode and surfed the boat's wake. We leaped in and out of the water with exuberant joy. This was the best dolphin fun I have had in a long time!

We performed acrobatic twists and flips to greet the sailors onboard. The crew, surprised and delighted by our presence, watched in awe as our sleek dolphin bodies showcased our agility and gracefulness in the air. The sailors on the boat, sensing our friendly nature, decided to join in the interaction. They tossed small bits of fish into the water, creating a makeshift aquatic playground for all of us. With each perfectly timed jump, we effortlessly caught the treats mid-air, showcasing our intelligence and dexterity. The sailboat and its crew became enchanted by this unexpected encounter, forging a connection between their human world and our enchanting marine realm. On this day, we bridged the gap between the terrestrial and aquatic realms in a dance that transcended language and boundaries. It was a fleeting yet profound moment—a meeting of species at the bow of a boat.

And then, out of the corner of my eye, I spotted her. The water sparkled with sunlight, creating a dance of glimmers that mirrored the anticipation in the air. She was beautiful. With her sleek, silver-gray coat, she approached me gracefully, her eyes reflecting intelligence and curiosity. I swam towards her, and our paths converged in a perfect aquatic rendezvous. As we met, our eyes locked in a silent exchange of recognition. The two of us circled each other, communicating with clicks and whistles, creating a symphony that resonated through the underwater world.

I wanted to ask for her name but suddenly felt an unusual shyness. As if she could read my mind, she spoke up before I could say anything. My name is Marina," she said with a smile. Then she asked, "And what's your name?" I took a deep breath and replied, "My name is Dolphinea." We both smiled a dolphin smile at each other. She asked me, "Where is your pod? I don't see other dolphins with you. Are you alone?" I replied, "Although I like to explore and sometimes wander away from my family pod, I always return to them at the end of the day." She appeared to be relieved as a smile filled her eyes. She said, "I also enjoy exploring and discovering new ocean wonders. I'm a very curious dolphin," she said with a wink. I thought, Not only is she beautiful, but she is also witty! With a smile, a whistle, and a click, I tossed my head back, did a backflip, and came to rest vertically, floating face-to-face with her. I noticed that her eyes widened with surprise, and it was apparent to me that she felt impressed with what she saw.

She suggested, "Let's swim and explore together, but I need to be back at sunset to rejoin my pod. I'm sure you'll need to get back to your pod too, right?" I agreed, "Yes, that's true." She expressed her joy, "I'm so glad that my pod welcomed you and you joined us in bow-riding and acrobatics." Then she added, "Maybe you can introduce me to your pod sometime?" I responded, 'That would be wonderful. I would like that." We swam side by side, glancing at each other and moving in synchronized, rhythmic, fluid motions.

In the heart of the vast ocean expanse, two dolphins found each other as if drawn by an invisible force. The water sparkled with sunlight across Marina with her sleek, silver-gray coat and vivacious, daring, and playful spirit; and Dolphinea with his playful and adventurous nature and his energetic personality. Both dreamers of dreams and two hopeful thinkers came together in the warm, blue waters of a tropical ocean. Two extraordinary dolphins with unique personalities found themselves on a collision course of fate. The duo continued their day's journey together, exploring the depths of the ocean side by side.

We journeyed beneath the water's surface and explored the stunning coral reefs and mysterious caves. The sun's rays shone through the clear water, casting a beautiful glow on the underwater landscape. We swam gracefully through the intricate coral formations, marveling at their beauty and complexity, encountering schools of tropical fish and delicate sea anemones along the way. As we approached the entrance of a mysterious underwater cave, our curiosity intensified. With a side-way glance at each other and an effortless swish of our tails, we ventured into the dark abyss, where bio-luminescent organisms painted the walls with a soft, otherworldly glow. Together, we skillfully glided through the twisting, turning, maze-like passages, our echolocation guiding us with precision. Inside the cave, we discovered a hidden enclave teeming with marine life, from luminescent jellyfish to elusive seahorses.

Emerging from the cave, we continued our exploration of the coral reefs, engaging in playful acrobatics and synchronized swimming. We communicated with each other through a symphony of clicks and whistles, and we sang to each other, expressing our delight at the enchanting world we discovered. The coral reefs and caves became a canvas for our' aquatic ballet. We discovered a new watery playground that we would share with each other in the days ahead.

As the day began to wane and the sun dipped below the horizon, our friendship grew and became a testament to the magic that happens when two souls, even in the form of dolphins, find each other in the vastness of the sea. The setting sun began to cast a warm glow across the water.

Dolphinea and Marina discovered a shared love for exploration and vowed that together they would venture forward into underwater caves and navigate through intricate coral mazes, and their bond would grow stronger with each passing day. Their friendship would become a testament to the harmonious dance of the ocean's inhabitants. The union of Dolphinea's wisdom and Marina's exuberance would create a magical synergy beneath the surface. They made this promise to each other on this spot, on this day.

Marina could hear the members of her pod calling after her as they gathered to make the journey back to Coral Cove, where they would call home for the night. Dolphinea realized that it was getting late and that he had a long way to swim back to his pod. They both knew how much this day meant to them. Looking at Marina in the soft glow of the setting sun, Dolphinea said to her, "I will come to you tomorrow. We will go on an adventure together, and I will bring you to meet my family and pod members." Upon hearing this, Marina felt a warm comfort come over her, and she responded, "I would really love that, and thank you for such a beautiful day of exploring and sharing."

Marina and Dolphinea touched each other's pectoral fins and briefly brushed against the sides of each other's dolphin beaks as a sweet gesture of affection. Marina then turned and swam towards her family pod while Dolphinea watched her fade into the evening shadows. The sounds of clicks and whistles from the other dolphins also faded away, leaving only the gentle sounds of the calm waters around him. As he turned to begin the journey home, silence set in, save for the sound of his breathing, the rippling of water off his body as he swam, and the beating of his heart.

# ✎ CHAPTER TWO ✎

Marina is a playful and vibrant female Atlantic bottle-nose dolphin. She has a remarkable, sleek, and shimmering silver-gray coat that glistens beautifully under the sunlight as she gracefully glides through the azure waters of her ocean home. Her vibrant personality sets her apart from the other dolphins in her pod. She is characterized by a playful and inquisitive nature. Marina was born into a close-knit pod that revels in the crystal-clear waters of the warm Caribbean Sea. She has an exceptional level of intelligence, which is evident from her ability to solve complex problems and effectively communicate with her fellow pod members. She possesses an innate sense of curiosity that drives her to explore the vast depths of the ocean. During her adventures, she discovers new wonders and forms deep connections with the marine life around her.

An extraordinary acrobat known for her unparalleled finesse in leaping and twirling in the air, she is a standout performer during the playful displays that dolphins engage in, captivating the attention of onlookers and leaving a lasting impression with her agility and speed. From a young age, she quickly gained a reputation for her exuberant spirit and insatiable curiosity, which dazzled her fellow dolphins. Her sleek body was like a living work of art as she performed acrobatic flips and spins, slicing through the waves. During the sun-kissed days, she honed her echolocation skills and played intricate games of tag with her pod-mates, creating a harmonious symphony of clicks and whistles that echoed through the tropical paradise.

Marina is also a highly loyal member of her dolphin pod. She has a nurturing personality, especially towards younger dolphins, and works to create a sense of unity and camaraderie among the group. In the vast and diverse world of the ocean, Marina stands out as a charismatic and intelligent leader. Her presence has left a lasting impact on the underwater environment, which she considers her home. As she has matured, Marina has taken on more responsibility within the pod. She has assumed the role of a mentor and teacher to the younger dolphins in her pod. Marina understands the importance of passing on essential survival skills to the next generation. As she began her day before the sun rose, she thought to herself, "Today is a special day. I will take the younger dolphins in the pod to a special cove and teach them how to fish."

Marina's favorite lesson involves teaching the art of fishing to the curious and energetic younger dolphins. Guiding them to a secluded cove abundant with schools of fish, Marina demonstrates the graceful dance of precision and patience required to catch a meal. With fluid movements and swift flips of her powerful tail, she showcases the techniques of corralling and herding fish into a manageable cluster. The younger dolphins, their eyes wide with fascination, mimic Marina's every move as they learn the intricate choreography of the hunt. As the lessons progress, Marina not only imparts practical fishing skills but also emphasizes the importance of cooperation and communication among the pod. Through a symphony of clicks, whistles, and body language, she orchestrates a synchronized effort that enables the young dolphins to work together seamlessly. Under Marina's guidance, the once-inexperienced learners transform into a cohesive group of skilled hunters, ready to navigate the vast ocean and sustain their pod with the bounties it offers.

Marina addresses the group, saying, "My little ones, you have all done exceptionally well today, and I am very proud of each and every one of you." She adds, "Now you can work together as the perfect team to catch fish." She encourages them to keep practicing and honing their skills, as they have learned something crucial today as dolphins. Catching fish is essential for the survival and well-being of their pod. "It's time for us to leave this place and head back to the pod," she said. "Everyone is waiting for us to tell them the good news. Come along now, little ones." Marina and her students swam the short distance back to Coral Cove, where the rest of the pod was gathered.

As they arrived, it was already late morning and time for a meal. However, the young fishermen were not hungry, as they had already eaten their fill of the catch. There was a great sense of joy and excitement as the pod members welcomed them. The other dolphins clicked and whistled in a cheerful manner that could be heard miles away as the younger dolphins were congratulated and praised for their excellent work.

Marina's mother greeted her, saying, "My sweet, beautiful daughter. I am very proud of you for your unwavering commitment and devotion to the well-being of our pod. Thank you for teaching the little ones today. Our pod leader and his advisors have informed me that they value your loyalty and skills. They believe you will accomplish great things, and I share this belief as well." Marina responded, "Mother, I know there's something I am destined to do and someone I am destined to become someday. I feel it." Marina added, "I can't explain it, but I sense something. I think I'll understand it soon." Upon hearing this, Marina's mother nodded with that familiar look of understanding that she has shown to me and my siblings on many occasions.

Maris, Marina's mother, is an esteemed member and elder stateswoman of their pod. She is beautiful and regal, with fine lines etched into her sleek, silver-gray skin that bear the marks of countless adventures. Her dorsal fin, weathered by the currents of time, stands as a testament to her years of leading her family and pod through the vast expanses of the sea.

Maris' eyes, a deep and knowing indigo, hold a wisdom that transcends the language of the waves. They sparkle with the reflections of a myriad of tales, each ripple in her gaze telling a story of survival, love, and the eons of knowledge passed down through generations. Her sonorous clicks and whistles echo through the underwater canyons, carrying the weight of a lifetime's worth of communication and guidance. As an elder stateswoman of the pod, Maris moves with regal grace; her movements are measured and deliberate. Her once agile body now carries the gentle sway of experience, and every scar that adorns her form speaks of battles fought and alliances forged beneath the ever-changing surface of the ocean. The younger dolphins gather around her, seeking solace in the shadow of her wisdom, as Maris continues to navigate the currents of life with a profound understanding that only the vastness of time could bestow.

Maris excitedly informed Marina and the other young adult members of the pod that a scout had spotted human sailing vessels near Coral Cove. The entire pod would be moving within the hour to intercept the sailboats and enjoy some dolphin fun and merriment. Excitement and anticipation filled the air as the dolphins flapped their fins and tails, causing the water to froth and bubble. Upon arrival, they knew there would be jumping, acrobatics, and bow-riding by both the young and older adults. The humans might even toss a fish or two. The entire pod of dolphins gathered to swim towards the area where the sailboats had been spotted. They swam in perfect synchronization, with the male dolphins taking the lead and swimming alongside the group to protect them from harm. The females and younger members swam in the middle of the formation, while the elders and slower, older dolphins took up the rear. The pod leader, who made the decision to move the pod for the day's fun and adventure, was also in this rear conclave.

Marina swam ahead of the group with the males at her side. Since the males knew her strength, stamina, and acrobatic abilities, as well as her adventurous nature, none of them objected. She had proven her skills and agility on many occasions. Even when they playfully teased and chided her, Marina had no objections and would join in the fun, as she was wholeheartedly accepted by them. As the pod journeyed on, their sleek bodies sliced through the waves with effortless grace, and their dorsal fins cut through the water like knives.

In the distance, a sailboat appeared on the horizon, its white sails billowing in the gentle breeze. Marina and the dolphin group immediately altered their course and began swimming towards the approaching vessel. As the sailboat drew nearer, the dolphins began their displays of acrobatics with exuberant enthusiasm, leaping out of the water in synchronized arcs. Their joyous clicks and whistles echoed through the air, creating a symphony of sound. The group of young adult dolphins began bow-riding as the boat was cutting through the water. They would jump out of the water just in front of the bow with leaps and bounds. Marina was excited to be playing and frolicking in the blue ocean waters with her fellow dolphins. She darted in and out of the waves that the sailboat was leaving in its wake. Marina would jump out of the water and do somersaults and twists while joining in the chorus with clicks and whistles of her own.

The sailors on the vessel watched in awe as the dolphins approached, their movements synchronized like a choreographed dance. The air buzzed with excitement as the sailors marveled at the beauty of these intelligent creatures. As if drawn by an invisible force, the dolphins glided effortlessly alongside the sailboat, their bodies gleaming in the fading sunlight. The sailors could almost feel the joy emanating from the playful marine acrobats. Laughter echoed across the deck as crew members pointed and cheered, thoroughly captivated by the impromptu show.

The dolphins, seemingly attuned to the sailors' presence, began interacting with the boat in an enchanting display of curiosity. They darted in and out of the boat's wake, riding the gentle swells with grace and finesse. The sailors leaned over the sides, their hands trailing in the cool water, as they made fleeting connections with their marine counterparts. A particularly bold dolphin leaped high into the air, executing a perfect somersault before splashing back into the sea. The sailors, inspired by the exuberance of their aquatic companions, couldn't resist joining in the spectacle. Some climbed onto the boat's bow, stretching their arms in playful imitation of the dolphins' acrobatics. The connection between humans and dolphins transcended the boundaries of species. It was a dance of joy, a celebration of life and the boundless wonders of the ocean. The sailors couldn't help but feel a profound sense of unity with the natural world, as if the dolphins had invited them to share in the magic of the sea.

Marina and her companions were aware that they had awakened something magical and extraordinary in the sailors' hearts. She was confident that their playful interactions with the sailors would leave an indelible mark on them. Marina hoped that the sailors would share their experiences of spending peaceful and joyous moments with our pod of dolphins with their children and pass on their memories to future generations.

Marina turned her head towards the port side of the vessel and couldn't believe what she was seeing. In front of her, a magnificent male dolphin that she didn't recognize leaped high into the air and executed a perfect somersault before splashing back into the sea. His sleek silver-blue skin shimmered brilliantly in the sunlight like a fresh suit of armor. Marina was amazed by the dolphin's ability to jump so high and wondered how it was possible. Once again, she observed as the unfamiliar dolphin joined the male dolphins in her pod, flawlessly synchronizing with them as they bow-rode in unison. She couldn't help but wonder how this dolphin was able to synchronize so well with the others despite not being part of her pod's male alliance. She exclaimed to herself in amazement.

She wasn't sure how to react to what she was seeing, but somehow it felt right. She began smiling and giggling like a little girl. As she floated and bobbed in the warm waters, she couldn't help but admire his acrobatic moves. For a fleeting moment, she thought he noticed her as his sparkling eyes showed curiosity and fascination towards her. However, she wasn't entirely sure if he really did notice her or if it was just her imagination. Nevertheless, his fierce and adventurous eyes captivated her. "I must meet this young stranger," she whispered to herself.

Marina patiently waited for the male dolphins to move away. She let the currents carry her toward the unfamiliar male dolphin with caution. As they approached each other, Marina admired his sleek body and strong flippers. The male dolphin circled around her playfully, sparking curiosity in his intelligent eyes. Marina responded by circling around him also, her eyes fixed on his gaze. Marina broke the silence by introducing herself: "My name is Marina, and what is yours?" "My name is Dolphinea." He replied, They both smiled, and she asked him, "Where is your pod? I don't see other dolphins with you. Are you alone?" He replied, "Although I like to explore and sometimes wander away from my family pod, I always return to them at the end of the day." Marina was glad that she wasn't conversing with a rogue dolphin. He appeared to be a friendly, intelligent, and inquisitive creature. She was pleased to know that he had a family and was part of a dolphin pod, just like she was. This made her feel secure.

Dolphinea began to showcase his agility, performing acrobatic leaps and spins. She knew he wanted to impress her and demonstrate his strength and grace. He flipped onto his back, revealing his pale belly—the equivalent of a dolphin smile. Marina watched this display, her eyes softening. She appreciated his efforts but had to remind herself that she was not a passive observer. She, too, began to do swirls in the water, showing off her speed and finesse. Marina said, "I also enjoy exploring and discovering new ocean wonders. I'm a curious dolphin, and she gave Dolphinea a wink. "Let's swim and explore together." Dolphinea smiled at Marina and nodded his approval. They agreed to return before sunset so Marina could rejoin her pod and Dolphinea could make the journey home to his family. They swam side by side, their bodies occasionally brushing against each other—a dance of exploration, a delicate balance between curiosity and caution.

Marina and Dolphinea went on an enchanting journey through a maze of underwater caves and colorful coral reefs. Their streamlined bodies effortlessly glided through the crystal-clear waters as they explored the mysterious darkness of the caves. Inside the caverns, they discovered a hidden and magical world. Exploring the depths of the underwater caves unveils a mesmerizing spectacle of iridescence dancing along the walls, casting an otherworldly glow upon the surrounding darkness. These caves, a testament to nature's artistic prowess, harbor passages, and corridors adorned with vibrant hues that seem to shift and shimmer with every subtle movement of the water. Some of these passages are narrow and winding, compelling the two explorers to navigate in a single file, relying on each other as beacons of guidance through the labyrinthine twists and turns. In this mysterious realm, teamwork becomes essential as the two companions forge ahead; their silhouettes illuminate their path, creating an ethereal symphony of light and shadow in the watery depths.

Dolphinea reminisced, telling Marina the tales his Uncle Jinn used to tell him about the caves he grew up exploring in the Far East. Marina listened attentively to these strange tales with curiosity and amazement. Emerging from the mysterious caves, the two dolphins turned their attention to the kaleidoscopic coral reefs that painted the ocean floor with a breathtaking display of colors. Brilliant shades of red, orange, and yellow dance alongside the soft pastels of pink and lavender, painting a stunning tapestry against the azure backdrop of the sea. Emerald greens blend seamlessly with the rich blues of the ocean, while bursts of neon hues from fish and other marine creatures add flashes of electric excitement.

Underneath it all, the corals come alive in various hues, from the warm golden tones of healthy coral to the muted purples and blues of those in shadow. In this bustling metropolis by the sea, every color tells a story, and every shade is a testament to the beauty and diversity thriving within this underwater wonderland. As the duo swam gracefully amid the coral gardens, their inquisitive eyes scanned the intricate structures, home to many marine life. Schools of iridescent fish darted around them, seeking refuge in the protective embrace of the coral.

In this underwater paradise, they engaged in a curious dance, exploring the coral reefs' nooks and crannies with unparalleled grace. Their synchronized movements revealed a profound connection as they navigated through the underwater tapestry, weaving in and out of the living sculptures created by millennia of natural artistry. Marina felt a closeness with Dolphinea she had not felt with anyone else. She truly found herself captivated by this stranger. Their playful interactions during underwater exploration, gentle games, and synchronized swimming brought a spark between them that she could not deny.

Leaving the enchanted forest of living coral reefs, Marina and Dolphinea ascended toward the surface, a dance of elegance unfolding beneath the fading light of the day. Together, they breached the surface in perfect unison, their dorsal fins slicing through the air like crescent moons. As they broke free into the open expanse, a canvas of hues painted the sky above, transitioning from the vibrant blues of the deep sea to the warm, glowing embrace of the setting sun. With a synchronized leap, they emerged from the water, their eyes reflecting the kaleidoscope of colors that adorned the horizon. Silhouetted against the backdrop of the descending sun, they appeared to be momentarily suspended in time, bathed in an ethereal glow.

Marina felt a deep connection with Dolphinea and cherished their shared moments. She knew there was much to learn about him. She prayed they would meet again to explore the ocean's wonders and discuss their future together. As they floated on the water's surface, basking in the sunset's golden glow, Marina heard her pod calling out to her. They were gathering to return to Coral Cove for the night. Dolphinea noticed the time and turned to Marina. He said, "I will come to you tomorrow. We will go on an adventure together, and I will introduce you to my family and pod members." Marina replied, "Yes, I would like that very much." Marina was pleased about that and gave Dolphinea directions to Coral Cove.

Dolphinea knew that, because of his keen sense of direction and his echolocation skills, he would have no problem finding his way there. Marina felt a warm comfort wash over her as Dolphinea touched her pectoral fin gently and briefly brushed his dolphin beak against hers. With that, Marina turned and swam the short distance to rejoin her pod. She was tempted to look back but resisted, wanting to preserve the moment and keep it close to her heart until they met again.

# ❧ CHAPTER THREE ❧

Dolphinea's day began early, as the sun rose in the east and the waters were still and calm. Although he returned to the pod late the night before, he was full of energy and anticipation this morning. Typically, Dolphinea only sleeps for a few hours at a time, but during that time, he can shut down half of his brain, along with the opposite eye. The other half of his brain stays awake at a low level of alertness to watch for predators, obstacles, and other ocean creatures. It also signals when to rise to the surface for fresh air. After about two hours, he will reverse this process, resting the active side of his brain and waking the rested half. This pattern is also known as cat-napping.

He sometimes enters a deeper form of sleep, mainly during the night. This state is called logging because it resembles a log floating on the water's surface. Dolphinea likes to catch a wink or two by resting quietly in the water vertically or horizontally or while swimming slowly alongside another dolphin. Due to his adventurous nature, he does this frequently while swimming with the pod. Today, he feels well-rested and prepared for the day's adventures.

Some of the other males in the pod are also waking up. They began to gather around him. They are Sol, Xenios, Nova, Medea, and Cersei. These are Dolphinea's best friends and lifelong members of his male alliance. They greet each other cheerfully, as they have on many mornings, with the clicks and whistles that good friends use. They communicate their intentions and weave intricate social bonds in their early-morning liquid playground. As the sun rises and casts its golden hues upon the surface, they engage in a spirited game of chase, racing each other with youthful energy. As the playtime unfolds and they continue their jovial antics, the call of hunger beckons. Dolphinea turns to Sol and the others and asks, "Are you ready for some morning hunting?" They all respond in unison, "Absolutely." Then Sol says, "We've been eager to dive into the hunt since dawn broke." They wonder what's on the menu today. Dolphinea says, "I saw a school of mackerel near the coral reef. They seem quite abundant today, perfect for a satisfying breakfast." "They're fast swimmers, though. We'll need to coordinate our movements to herd them effectively." Sol answers for the group, "Sounds like a plan. Ready when you are, Dolphinea. Let's make this morning hunt a success!" They all set off for the coral reef.

The young male adults gracefully cut through the glassy morning sea as they embarked on their hunting expedition. Their sleek bodies glided effortlessly through the water, and their movements synchronized perfectly. With learned precision, the dolphins seamlessly transition from play to hunt. Dolphinea takes the lead, his keen senses detecting the telltale signs of the prey nearby. Sol, ever vigilant, positions himself strategically, ready to assist in herding their quarry towards the shallows. The other hunters take up their respective positions. With precision and coordination born from years of experience, they execute their plan flawlessly, corralling a school of mackerel with finesse and skill. Together, they dart and weave through the water, their teamwork a testament to the bond forged through countless hunts shared beneath the waves. Like a well-oiled machine, they execute their strategy, herding the panicked fish into tighter formations with strategic leaps and dives.

The ocean briefly erupts in a symphony of splashes and echoes as they celebrate their successful hunt, their jubilant whistles echoing across the vast expanse of the sea. With their bellies full and spirits high, the tight-knit group of dolphin friends encircles the remaining school of mackerel. Coordinating their movements with silent understanding, they herd and drive their catch towards the waiting pod, providing breakfast for the rest of the pod members. The six friends continue their playful antics, weaving through the waves as inseparable companions in the timeless dance of life beneath the surface.

Dolphinea broke away from the group. He bowed his head in admiration and said, "See you all later." With a wave of his pectoral fin, he took one more leap, turned, and headed off to say good morning to his parents and siblings. The friends waved goodbye to him, clicking and whistling their appreciation for a great hunt. As he approached his family, he whistled a sweet dolphin good morning song that they recognized as his. His parents greeted him with smiles and clicks while his younger siblings giggled, laughed, and beamed with joy at his presence. Dolphinea's mother, Luna, spoke, "My, you are in a good mood this morning, my son." "There's a gleam in your eyes." Dolphinea shared, "Yesterday, during my afternoon adventure, I met Marina, the most beautiful and talented female dolphin I've ever seen. She and her pod are currently residing at Coral Cove." Luna smiled at him, and Dolphinea's father gave him that look that fathers give to their dolphin sons when they speak of female dolphins—a mixture of amusement, wisdom, and perhaps a hint of nostalgia. It was a glance that conveyed a silent understanding of the complexities of courtship and the pursuit of companionship beneath the waves.

Luna told her son, "I'm glad you've made a new female friend." Dolphinea said, "She is unique and unlike any other female I've met. She shares my playful and adventurous nature. We went on adventures together, exploring caves and coral reefs, singing, and frolicking in the ocean until sunset." Dolphinea's father, Delphin, after whom he was named, chuckled and said, "Luna, I think he's found the one!" Luna also laughed and said, "I think so, too." Dolphinea eagerly announced to his parents that he had plans to meet with Marina that day and was excited to introduce her to them, but only with their kind permission. He knew they would be thrilled to meet her, and he hoped they would welcome her with open arms. Dolphinea's parents nodded their approval.

Dolphinea and his father took a light swim together. During a private conversation between Delphin and Dolphinea, they exchanged chirps and clicks about the females' graceful movements and mesmerizing songs, including Delphin's beloved Luna. They both shared a bond of admiration for the mysterious allure of the opposite sex, which transcends the boundaries of species and echoes through the timeless rhythms of the ocean. Delphin validated and acknowledged Dolphinea's feelings for Marina and the universal experience of longing and desire.

Then Dolphinea had a nice swim with his mother. Luna spoke to him about the importance of finding the right female dolphin, with a mixture of tenderness and wisdom. As they swam side by side, her gentle chirps carried words of guidance and encouragement, emphasizing the significance of compatibility, mutual respect, and emotional connection in forging lasting bonds beneath the waves. With each graceful movement, she imparted lessons learned from her own experiences, instilling in him a deep appreciation for the complexities of relationships in the vast oceanic world they inhabited. Her words resonated with the warmth of maternal love, reminding him that the journey to finding a suitable mate was not just about physical attraction but also about shared values, understanding, and trust. In the depths of their aquatic realm, amidst the gentle sway of seaweed and the soft murmur of currents, his mother's counsel echoed like a guiding beacon, lighting the path toward a future filled with companionship and love. With joy and optimism swelling in his heart, Dolphinea swam towards Coral Cove to meet Marina.

Marina woke up to the sounds of young dolphins playing and laughing while they swam and played tag with each other. The day was dawning, and the sun and tropical water felt warm and inviting against her skin. Marina was excited to recount the events of the previous day. On their way back to Coral Cove, she shared with her mother, Maris, about her new friend Dolphinea and all their adventures. Maris had noticed the two of them together and was happy that Marina had found a companion to share her adventures with. Maris also shared that some of the male dolphins in the pod liked Dolphinea and welcomed him as part of their group whenever he visited. Maris was happy to hear that Dolphinea had a family and was part of a pod, which Marina confirmed.

Marina had developed intense emotions for Dolphinea but decided to keep them hidden. However, she suspected that her mother, Maris, was already aware of her feelings. As an elder stateswoman, Maris was wise in the ways of the dolphin realm, mainly regarding heart matters. Marina informed Maris that Dolphinea had said he would come to Coral Cove, and they would swim together to meet his pod and family. Upon hearing this, Maris was pleased. "Today is the day!" Marina thought to herself, brimming with excitement. She wondered why she should even try to hold back. After all, this incredibly handsome, athletic, and adventurous male dolphin shared her interests and seemed genuine in his affection for her. There was something about him that she just could not put into words—a magical and mysterious quality that drew her in. Little did she know that their adventure had just begun, and their paths crossing was not a random chance or coincidence. The future holds a special place for both of them; together, they will fulfill their destinies.

Marina had a breakfast of shrimp and some small crabs that she foraged off the coral beds. The male dolphins were out hunting this morning and would bring a school of herring or mackerel to the pod, but she was not that hungry this morning. Instead, she would exercise and do some tail fin (fluke) thrusts. I use my fluke for propulsion and also for communication. Moving my fluke up and down helps me swim efficiently, and I can even stun fish when striking them with it. It is also an excellent tool to use for defense. It can be very powerful when needed because of the muscular peduncle region that attaches it directly to my body. Sometimes, I use it to communicate by splashing it up and down in the water. It certainly helps me get the attention of other dolphins. I can increase my speed and agility by simultaneously exercising my tail-fin and body.

Marina gracefully propels herself through the water using her powerful tail fin. She navigates effortlessly with each fluid motion, displaying agility and strength. Her tail fin, a marvel of evolutionary design, propels her forward with precision and speed, allowing her to glide through the ocean gracefully and elegantly. Whether swimming alongside her pod or performing acrobatic feats, Marina's mastery of her tail fin helps her stand out above the other male and female dolphins in her pod.

After completing her exercises, Marina effortlessly floated atop the tranquil surface of the ocean, basking in the warmth of the sun's rays. With a graceful arch of her back, she seemed to embody serenity, her smooth movements reflecting a sense of ease and contentment. With her eyes closed, Marina appeared lost in a world of peaceful solitude, embracing the serenity of the vast expanse surrounding her. Each rise and fall of her breath was a rhythmic melody in harmony with the gentle sway of the water, as if the ocean itself were cradling her in its loving embrace. The sound of excited clicks and whistles from the edges of the pod brought her back into the present. Her curiosity dictated that she investigate the commotion. Marina began to swim over to where she had heard the sounds.

Dolphinea followed Marina's instructions from the day before and arrived at Coral Cove. He spotted her pod and cautiously approached, not wanting to startle them. He was still determining what kind of reception to expect. The area where the sailboat was sailing yesterday was full of playfulness and joy, but today, the pod was in their safe zone. The male members constantly watched, protecting the pod from predators, including rogue male dolphins. As he got closer, he could hear the enthusiastic clicks and whistles of the younger members of the pod. Two young male adults swam out to greet him, but they seemed to be cautious at first. However, when one of them recognized Dolphinea from the previous day, their behavior shifted from being careful to being relieved. Jasper was the first to speak, and he greeted Dolphinea by saying, "Welcome to our Coral Cove home, Dolphinea." The previous day, while bow-riding with some of the other males from Marina's pod, they exchanged names. Dolphinea responded, "Thank you; great to see you, Jasper. I am here by invitation from Marina." Jasper smiled and replied, "A friend of Marina's is always welcome, and you don't need an invitation. Our alliance has accepted you and you are always welcome." Dolphinea thanked Jasper and the other male, and they joined the rest of the pod.

A group of particularly curious juveniles caught sight of Dolphinea and his massive, muscular presence, gliding gracefully through the waves. Intrigued by his size and demeanor, they formed a tight circle around him, their curious eyes sparkling with wonder. Eager to learn from the experienced elder, they darted back and forth, chirping and clicking in excitement as they observed his every move. Accustomed to the youthful exuberance of these new companions, Dolphinea welcomed their attention with a patient smile. He slowed, allowing the young dolphins to swim closer and examine him with their playful nudges and gentle touches. With each graceful maneuver, he demonstrated the art of navigation and communication, inspiring his curious audience to mimic his movements in a joyous display of camaraderie.

Dolphinea also noticed a small group of females watching him. He watched as they smiled and giggled among themselves, darting their eyes toward him and then looking away. They pretended that they had no interest but were unable to avert their eyes for too long. He smiled as he remembered the conversation with his father earlier that day, particularly the part about the mysterious allure of the opposite sex and the mesmerizing songs of females. Today, his heart and attention were solely focused on Marina.

After all the excitement and enthusiasm surrounding his arrival dissipated and calmness returned to the pod, he spotted Marina swimming towards him. Their eyes met, and he approached her. They lost the distance between them until their noses met tenderly and intimately. In that fleeting touch, time seemed to stand still, the world around them fading into a blur of vibrant colors and whispers of the sea. Their connection was instant and profound, a silent understanding transcending language and boundaries. In that shared moment, Marina and Dolphinea experienced the same solace they felt the day before.

"Welcome to our home; I'm delighted you're here," Marina greeted me. "I'm pleased to be here too," Dolphinea responded. "I told my parents about you and our adventures yesterday. They would love to meet you," Dolphinea added. "Dolphinea continued, "It is so good to see you." "And you too," Marina replied. He asked, "Shall we swim to my pod, and I can introduce you to my parents?" Marina replied, "Yes, I would like that, but before we leave, let me introduce you to my mother, Maris." Dolphinea replied, "Yes. I would like that very much." Marina and Dolphinea swam together, following her guidance, to where her mother was waiting. As they swam, Dolphinea felt a deep connection with Marina—they were kindred spirits. He admired Marina's beauty and radiance, and he could sense their hearts fluttering with every graceful move forward they made.

Eager to meet Marina's mother and learn from her wisdom, Dolphinea and Marina spotted Maris gracefully swimming with a small group of dolphins, her presence exuding a sense of tranquility and authority. Marina had spoken highly of her mother's nurturing nature and deep understanding of the ocean's mysteries, and as Dolphinea drew closer, he felt a sense of reverence towards Maris. Marina introduced Dolphinea to her mother, Maris. In the company of Marina's mother, Dolphinea felt a deep sense of belonging and admiration. Maris shared stories of their dolphin heritage, passing down ancient wisdom and teaching Dolphinea the intricacies of their underwater world. Through their interactions, Dolphinea gained a newfound appreciation for their marine community and the importance of preserving their ocean home for future generations.

Maris gazed at Marina with a smile that conveyed her approval of Dolphinea. She thought this male dolphin might be the one they had been searching for. He was the only one who could help her daughter fulfill her destiny. Marina told Maris that she and Dolphinea planned to swim to Dolphinea's pod to meet his parents today. She also mentioned that they might return late. Maris knew that Marina would be safe with Dolphinea and his family, so she reassured them not to worry about returning at a specific time. Maris wished them a safe journey and blessed them before swimming back to her previous group of dolphins.

As Marina and Dolphinea start their journey back to Dolphinea's pod, the ocean stretches endlessly around them, its vastness both awe-inspiring and comforting. The sun casts a warm glow over the water's surface, creating a shimmering pathway that dances with every ripple. The two friends glide effortlessly through the clear blue depths, their sleek bodies cutting through the water gracefully and precisely.

Marina's heart swells with gratitude for the friendship she shares with Dolphinea. She feels so grateful that they met and looks forward to exploring the ocean's wonders together and sharing countless adventures. Dolphinea's playful spirit and boundless enthusiasm lift Marina's spirits, and she's grateful for the companionship and support they offer each other.

Marina and Dolphinea pass by vibrant coral reefs teeming with life as they swim. Schools of colorful fish dart in and out of the coral, their scales glinting in the sunlight. Sea turtles lazily glide by, their ancient wisdom evident in the steady rhythm of their movements. Everywhere they look, the ocean is alive with beauty and wonder.

Despite the distance still to travel, Marina feels a sense of peace settling over her. With Dolphinea by her side, she knows they can overcome any challenge that comes their way. Together, they'll navigate the currents, brave the depths, and return safely to Dolphinea's pod, where they'll share their tales of adventure and laughter with his family and friends and with her family and friends when they return to her pod. As they continue their journey, Marina and Dolphinea's bond grows stronger.

# ❧ CHAPTER FOUR ❧

Dolphinea estimated that the distance from Coral Cove to his pod was about thirty miles. He could usually complete the journey in just over two hours due to his speed and agility. However, since he was with Marina, he wanted to take it slow and enjoy the scenery while conversing. The distance an individual dolphin travels from the main group varies depending on the pod's rules and customs. The home range of most dolphins in our pod is usually less than thirty miles, with much of our time spent in an even smaller core area. The Coral Cove is at the edge of my pod's core range. Of course, our pods move from one place to another, and as a group, we have been known to travel eighty miles in a single day.

As an adventurer, I have traveled well beyond the thirty-mile limit in a single day on numerous occasions. Today, Marina and I are undertaking a relatively easy swim between our respective pods. I assured her that we would keep a comfortable cruising speed and should reach my pod in about three hours, considering rest breaks, current changes, and variations in our swimming abilities. Marina proved to be a skilled and agile swimmer, keeping up with me easily. The ocean was calm today, so we used short bursts of energy to increase our speed. The exhilarating water inspired us to keep up a steady pace.

As Dolphinea and Marina glided effortlessly through the crystal-clear waters of the ocean, they saw a breathtaking sight: sea turtles gracefully swimming through the water. The turtles' shells were adorned with intricate patterns that sparkled in the sunlight. The dolphins watched in awe as the turtles moved with serene elegance, their movements graceful and fluid. The sea turtles seem unfazed by the dolphin couple's presence, continuing their unhurried journey through the ocean's depths. As they continued on their journey, they came across a fantastic sight. A group of manta rays glided gracefully through the water, their elegant wings undulating with each fluid movement. Dolphinea and Marina were captivated by the mesmerizing ballet of these majestic creatures. They joined and swam alongside them, creating a harmonious display of marine beauty. Together, they created an enchanting scene beneath the waves.

The two dolphins came across a beautiful island halfway through their journey. They decided to change course and head towards it. As they approached the island, they saw that the surrounding waters were full of fish and marine life. The waters were shallow, with rocky cliffs on one side of the island, while the beaches were covered in pristine white sand. They also noticed some coves that would serve as good shelter at night. The dolphins agreed to explore this new island sanctuary when they had more time, but they headed back towards Dolphinea's pod for now.

The tropical waters were teeming with marine life today, and they marveled at how fortunate they were to share such sights. While swimming together, they shared stories about their childhood memories and the games they used to play with other dolphins in their pods. They compared the lessons they learned while growing up and discussed the challenges they had to overcome as young adults. Dolphinea shared with Marina the complex bond he shares with his male dolphin friends. They have faced many battles and gone on many hunts together. Marina was aware that male dolphins form alliances to cooperate with each other, specifically to help find females to mate with and herd, and they also assist in stealing females from other male dolphins. She has always believed that most male dolphins display aggressive and polygamous behavior, especially regarding mating.

As a female dolphin, she has experienced firsthand male dolphins' aggressive and competitive behavior during the breeding season. She has witnessed how males chase and violently attack females, using their tails, heads, and bodies to hit, bite, and slam into them. This kind of behavior is not only distressing but also abusive. She shudders when recalling the mistreatment and aggression she has suffered at the hands of some males in her pod. Dolphinea noticed Marina was uneasy, so he moved closer to her. He knew it wasn't the right moment to discuss his male connections with her. Instead, he reassured her he wasn't like the other males she may have encountered. His words brought her relief, and she trusted him. "Today is a day for adventure and good times!" He said it in a playful voice. Marina cheerfully laughed at his words as they swam together.

Swimming side by side, their sleek bodies slicing through the water easily, they spotted a mother whale and her calf gliding serenely through the currents just ahead. Pausing in their synchronized swim, Dolphinea and Marina approached the gentle giants with curiosity and respect. The mother whale, towering yet gentle, guided her calf with nurturing care, a testament to the enduring bond between parent and child in the vast blue world beneath the waves.

The dolphins swam alongside them, sharing a moment of quiet awe before continuing their journey, leaving a scene of tranquil beauty in the endless expanse of the ocean. This is precisely what they both needed to experience at that moment. It was as if the universe knew this and had embraced the couple in a warm and nurturing way. The sight of the mother and her calf grounded their thoughts and warmed their hearts as they swam the last few miles of their journey.

Dolphinea and Marina heard the distant sounds of dolphins as they approached his pod.

Their excitement and anticipation grew as they got closer. Two male dolphins swam out to greet them, just like the two males from Marina's pod had done earlier that morning when Dolphinea approached the perimeter of the Coral Cove. Dolphinea immediately recognized these males, Sol and Cersei, as his good friends. Both males recognized Dolphinea and shouted ahead of them, "Dolphinea, we're so glad you're back. We've got some important things to tell you." As they arrived, he could hear the urgency in their voices and feel their fast breathing, causing the water around them to bubble. After Sol and Cersei caught their breath, they both yelled in unison, "Sharks!" Dolphinea's heart began to race. Marina retreated behind his back and tucked her nose into Dolphinea's dorsal fin.

Indeed, sharks are often regarded as some of the most dangerous predators that dolphins face, particularly in regions like the Caribbean and the southern Atlantic coasts, where both of us inhabit. Among the various species of sharks, the tiger shark stands out as a significant threat to us dolphins; we are among their favored prey. Being highly intelligent and social, we have developed strategies to mitigate the risk that sharks pose to us. That is why we live and travel in pods, which enhances our safety through our numbers. Growing up in our pods, we have learned defensive techniques such as forming tight groups and alliances or using coordinated movements to fend off shark attacks. Despite these strategies, interactions between our pods and sharks can still be intense and sometimes fatal for us dolphins, especially for our weaker members.

Sometimes, they don't always intend to kill us for food. Sometimes, they want to defend what they consider their territory, but sometimes, they come and attack in groups to gain territory or because they are predatory fish that pose a problem for us. It is hard to predict their behavior before they strike. Sharks rely heavily on their instincts, and they tend to react opportunistically and without much concern for their safety, especially when they detect the scent of blood or vibrations in the water caused by a struggling creature that could be their prey. Scars received on our skin by sharks indicate that the bite marks are evidence that sharks strike from below and behind us and see us as prey. Both sharks and dolphins are considered apex predators in the ocean environment and, for the most part, swim clear of each other. Usually, when sharks spot a group of dolphins, they will flee. But not always.

Cersei has had many battles with sharks and has the scars to show. Once, he was bitten so severely by a shark attack that we didn't think he would make it. It took many months for him to heal, and we cared for him and nurtured him until he was strong again. Our bond is unbreakable. He is both my friend and my protector. Our pod members respect him and consider him an expert in shark behavior and strategies to defeat them. I am glad he is here to greet us and guide us into the safety of my pod.

Dolphinea and Marina, flanked by Sol and Cersei, made their way into the main body of the pod. Adult male dolphins patrolled the perimeters, constantly looking out for tiger sharks, which convinced Dolphinea that this was serious business this time. Dolphinea thanked his two brave friends and introduced them to Marina within the pod's safety. The two strong males were pleased to meet her, and they both fell back, showing her their pale white bellies as a sign of acceptance and vulnerability towards her. The first time she saw this behavior was when Dolphinea did that when they first met. She was unfamiliar with this new behavior, but it made her feel comfortable and safe. What an odd group of males! She thought, but I like them!

Sol turned to Dolphinea and said, "There will be a group meeting in a couple of hours to discuss the shark situation and how the pod will deal with this threat, including how we will dispatch them." Dolphinea replied, "I will be there, but first, I must introduce Marina to my parents and family. I will see you at the meeting." The two male protectors swam away to organize the meeting, while Dolphinea and Marina went to find his family.

Luna, the embodiment of grace and with wisdom etched in the lines around her eyes, was conversing with a group of other female dolphins. Luna's presence within the group commanded respect and admiration. As Dolphinea and Marina approached the group, Luna turned to them. She greeted her son and his new female friend with a smile of relief and admiration. She warmly welcomed Marina into the group and dismissed Dolphinea, saying, "Go to your meeting, my son, and come back to us afterward. Marina and I have much to discuss. She will remain by my side until your return." Dolphinea thanked his mother, Luna, and gently brushed against her and Marina's pectoral fins. He turned and left to rejoin the other male dolphins in his alliance.

Marina watched as the wise Luna began communicating with the group with gentle clicks and whistles. Her melodic voice carried the weight of years of experience and understanding. Her tales of navigating the vast ocean, raising offspring, and forming bonds with other marine creatures resonated deeply with each of us, inspiring a sense of unity and kinship among the group. Listening intently, we hung on every word Luna spoke, her anecdotes weaving a tapestry of shared history and collective wisdom. Her guidance and counsel were invaluable as we faced the challenges of our marine world, especially as we face today's shark challenges. She offered perspectives shaped by a lifetime of observation and learning.

Luna's presence reminded all of us of the importance of cherishing our connections, respecting our environment, and embracing the legacy of those who came before us. As the conversation unfolded, it was clear that Luna's wisdom would continue to guide and inspire us, echoing through the waves long after our gathering had ended. We discussed the threat the pod faces from the unusual behavior of the tiger sharks. Luna conjectured that something else was going on that must be driving the sharks to gather around and threaten our pod. Something besides hunger and dominance has brought them to the edges of our pod these days. When the male adults devise a strategy to dispatch the tiger sharks, and the elders present it to our leader, the answer to why they are swarming around our pod and territory will become clear. She reassured us that the wisest of our elders will come together to discuss this present phenomenon.

Dolphinea joined the other male dolphins at the gathering to discuss the threat of the tiger sharks to the pod. The group speculated on the reasons behind the sudden influx of sharks, pondering whether it was due to changes in prey availability or shifts in ocean currents. Regardless of the cause, the dolphins knew they must remain vigilant to safeguard their pod's safety.

Sol spoke first. "I have noticed," Sol began, his voice carrying the weight of experience, "that these sharks are not merely solitary hunters but are gathering in groups, six to twelve strong. This is a concerning development, indicating a coordinated effort in response to the changing currents and food shortages further to the north. His words hung heavy in the water as the males exchanged worried glances, the realization sinking in that the threat they faced was not merely individual predators but a formidable coalition of hunters. "Have you felt the change in the currents?" murmured Taran, one of the oldest male dolphins among them, his voice tinged with a hint of sadness. "It's as if the very heartbeat of the ocean is shifting, drawing these predators closer to our home." A murmur of concern rippled through the group as they exchanged knowing glances.

Dolphinea spoke up. "I think it is important for us to bring this information to the elders and share our plan to help defend the pod against the tiger sharks while the elders develop a more permanent solution." The group of males nodded in agreement. Dolphinea added, "On our way back to the pod today, Marina and I noticed a small island. As we approached the island, we saw that the surrounding waters were full of fish and marine life. The waters were shallow, and rocky cliffs were on one side of the island. We also noticed some coves that would serve as good shelter at night. And the good news is that there were no sharks around the island." With a chorus of affirmative clicks, whistles, and nods of relief, the male dolphins agreed to bring this news to the elders. Taran added, "We must remain vigilant! Together, we shall devise strategies to navigate these treacherous waters and safeguard our pod against this new threat." As the discussion continued, the dolphins reaffirmed their bond and solidarity, determined to defend their territory and loved ones at all costs. They outlined plans to increase patrols around the perimeter of their pod's territory, utilizing their superior speed and agility to keep potential predators at bay.

Dolphinea and Taran were chosen to meet with the elders, as the others in the group, with a keen sense of strategy, decided to split into three teams, each tasked with hunting down the encroaching predators. Led by Sol, Medea, and Cersei, the teams embarked on their mission with steely determination, their sleek bodies slicing through the water with purpose. Sol's team, known for their strategic prowess, set off towards the northern boundary, where the tiger sharks were most prevalent. With Sol's steady leadership guiding them, they forged ahead, their keen senses alert for any sign of danger lurking beneath the waves. Meanwhile, Medea's team ventured towards the eastern flank, where the currents ran swift and treacherous. With their powerful tails propelling them forward, they scanned the waters with unwavering focus, ready to confront any threat that dared to challenge their domain.

At the same time, Cersei's team charted a course toward the southern depths, where the shadows of the deeper waters concealed unknown dangers. With Cersei's fearless spirit leading the way, they plunged into the murky depths, their clicks and whistles echoing through the darkness as they prepared to face whatever lay ahead. Together, these three teams of male dolphins embarked on their mission, bound by a common purpose: to protect their pod and preserve the fragile harmony of their underwater world.

# ❧ CHAPTER FIVE ❧

In the early afternoon, the Caribbean Ocean is a dazzling display of azure waters stretching endlessly beneath the tropical sun. The warm tropical breeze carries the scent of salt and seaweed, while the distant sound of seagulls adds to the symphony of the sea. In this tranquil moment, amid the vastness of the Caribbean, time seemed to stand still, allowing dolphins and other sea inhabitants to savor life's simple pleasures beneath the sun-kissed waves. Today, however, a subtle uneasiness permeates the air within the dolphin pod. Despite the radiant sunshine and the sparkling clarity of the ocean, there's a palpable shift in the pod's demeanor, a departure from their usual carefree antics. The presence of a predator lurking nearby casts a shadow of fear over the usually tranquil waters. Despite the uneasiness in the air, there's also a resilience within the pod, a quiet determination to weather whatever challenges come their way. In this moment of uncertainty, the bond between Marina, Luna, and the other female dolphins grows stronger, their shared experience forging a more profound sense of camaraderie.

The elders have called an assembly, and Luna has been summoned to join them. Luna has permitted Marina to join them as an observer since she is a guest of Luna and her son, Dolphinea.

Luna is told that Dolphinea will also be in attendance. Since Delphin, Dolphinea's father, is an elder statesman, he will attend. Besides the others in attendance, most of the pod members will remain in groups, huddling close together within the safety of the pod structure inside the boundaries to the open sea. Within the hierarchy of the pod, the elders will advise, and the leader will make the final decision on what course of action will be taken. At that time, all the members of the pod that are able and present will come together for his proclamation.

Marina feels both excited and honored to be a part of this pod's dolphin assembly, which has been convened to decide upon the laws and actions governing their pod. Back in her pod, she has not yet been privileged to attend. However, she understands they are much the same. The members begin to arrive and take up their proper places in a circular formation, with the elders positioned at the center, their wisdom and experience revered by all. Surrounding them are the invited attendees, each contributing their unique perspectives and insights to the discussion. Marina observes that the atmosphere is one of respect and solemnity. The group of elder dolphins convenes as the gentle currents swirl around them.

One of the eldest, a wise dolphin named Sylva, raised her voice above the murmurs of concern from those in attendance, her eyes reflecting the weight of their predicament. "My dear companions," Silva began, her tone somber yet determined, "We must face the reality of our changing ocean. The currents have shifted, bringing forth predators from distant waters seeking sustenance where once there was plenty." Nods of agreement rippled through the group as they pondered the implications of the encroaching threat. Another elder dolphin, a venerable patriarch named Ondar, spoke up with a voice that resonated with wisdom and compassion.

"Our strength lies in our unity and resilience," Ondar declared, echoing through the underwater realm. "Let us not yield to fear, but instead, let us adapt and persevere. Together, we shall find a way to navigate these turbulent waters and safeguard our pod." Nodding in agreement, Lyrion, another esteemed pod member, spoke up, his voice resonating with wisdom earned through years of experience. "The southward migration of the sharks is a symptom of a deeper imbalance in our ecosystem. With food becoming scarce in their native waters, they seek new hunting grounds, and unfortunately, we find ourselves in their path."

Marina noticed Luna glancing at a beautiful elder male dolphin with a sleek, silver-gray body adorned with subtle hues of pink and white. He had a strange face that she did not recognize as that of a bottle-nose dolphin. Luna nodded as if to encourage this elderly male to speak up. She noticed me watching and whispered that this dolphin was Dolphinea's uncle, Jinn. Marina remembered the tales Dolphinea had told her about his uncle. As if on cue and with a somber tone, Uncle Jinn spoke of the once vibrant coral reefs that had thrived in the embrace of warm, crystal-clear waters. "I have seen the coral reefs wither and die," Jinn lamented, his voice heavy with sorrow. "Once vibrant ecosystems are now reduced to barren wastelands, robbed of life by the ravages of ocean warming and pollution,"

The elders listened intently, their hearts heavy with the weight of Jinn's words. They knew that the health of the coral reefs was a barometer of the ocean's vitality, and their decline signaled a dire warning for all who called the sea their home. "The changes are not confined to the coral reefs alone," Jinn continued, his voice tinged with sadness. "I have witnessed the ebb and flow of ocean currents, shifting in unpredictable patterns, disrupting the delicate balance of life beneath the waves." Uncle Jinn spoke of the vast expanse of the North Atlantic, once a realm of icy splendor and powerful currents. "In my travels," Jinn continued, his voice carrying the weight of ancient knowledge, "I have witnessed ocean currents shifting in the North Atlantic, where mighty streams once flowed with unwavering strength. But now, these currents falter and wane, their paths disrupted by the warming embrace of changing climates."

As the elders of the pod listened intently, Jinn recounted the gradual retreat of once-majestic ice shelves, their icy fortresses melting away beneath the relentless assault of rising temperatures. "The ice shelves that once stood as guardians of the Arctic are disappearing," Jinn mourned, his voice tinged with sorrow. "Their loss not only reshapes the landscape of the frozen north but also heralds profound changes for the entire planet." In the depths of the ocean, where currents carve paths through the abyss and ice shelves stand as sentinels of the polar realms, the elders of the pod grappled with the magnitude of Jinn's words.

They knew that the changes unfolding in the North Atlantic were not merely a tale of distant lands but a harbinger of the challenges ahead for all who called the ocean home. And as they listened to Jinn's tales of currents shifting and ice shelves melting, they resolved to stand as guardians of the sea, united in their determination to protect and preserve the fragile balance of life beneath the waves.

Uncle Jinn ended his presentation with a message of hope. "The tides may be shifting, and the waters may seem uncertain, but we can restore balance and harmony to our marine world. In the face of rising temperatures and altering currents, it is easy to feel overwhelmed. But let us not lose heart. Instead, I know of a solution. There is a secret place hidden beneath the waves within an outcrop of caves in the waters east of Bimini that holds the key to restoring the delicate ecosystems that sustain us, from the coral reefs to the seagrass meadows. It is possible to restore the underwater streams to their natural flow." As Uncle Jinn's words echo through the waters, the elders and attendees gather closely, their eyes reflecting a mix of curiosity, determination, and hope as they absorb the wisdom of their elders.

As Luna addresses the gathered elders, her voice carries the weight of centuries of wisdom and experience. With a solemn yet hopeful tone, she recounts the remarkable tale of Dolphinea's and Marina's discovery of an island sanctuary during his return to the pod. With a sense of reverence, Luna describes how Dolphinea, guided by an unyielding sense of adventure and deep intuition, embarked on a solitary journey into uncharted waters. Through the ebb and flow of the ocean's currents, Dolphinea forged ahead, his spirit undeterred by the vastness of the unknown. As Luna paints a vivid picture of Dolphinea's voyage, the elders listen with rapt attention, their eyes reflecting a mix of wonder and admiration. They hang on every word, captivated by the tale of bravery and exploration unfolding before them. Luna speaks of how Dolphinea's relentless determination led him to stumble upon a hidden treasure—a pristine island sanctuary untouched by human hands.

With this knowledge, the assembly rejoiced, letting out whistles and clicks, fins splashing the water, and heads nodding in synchronized approval. Dolphinea came forward to face the circle of elders and spoke, "On our way back to the pod today, Marina and I noticed a small island. As we approached the island, we saw that the surrounding waters were full of fish and marine life. The waters were shallow, and rocky cliffs were on one side of the island. A blanket of pure white sand covers the beaches. We also noticed some coves that would serve as good shelter at night. There were no humans or sailing vessels in the waters around the island. And the good news is that there were no sharks! It is approximately twenty miles from our present location and an easy journey for the pod members. Marina and I can guide you there."

The elders agreed to discuss with the pod leader the possibility of relocating the pod to a new location due to the threat of predators, such as tiger sharks, converging on their home and feeding grounds. The elders asked Dolphinea and Taran what steps had been taken to deal with the tiger sharks. Taran explained that the male dolphins had formed three teams to hunt down the predators and were led by Sol, Medea, and Cersei. They had already begun their mission earlier that day. Taran and Dolphinea had stayed behind with a few allies to protect the pod. Their job was to defend against tiger sharks that might break through the dolphin safety net formed by the males patrolling outside the perimeter. The elders were pleased with this plan and showed their approval. They also decided to inform Kersus, their pod leader, about these details.

Uncle Jinn spoke up and reminded the other elders that he and the others should also discuss his message and proposal with Kersus. Silva, the elder, adjourned the assembly and dismissed the members in attendance. The next step is for the elders to meet with Kersus, their pod leader. Gathered beneath the shimmering surface of the Caribbean waters, the council of elder dolphins convenes with Kersus, their esteemed leader, to deliberate upon these matters of great importance. With profound reverence, the elders share their insights and concerns, their collective wisdom serving as a beacon of guidance for the pod. As Kersus listens intently to the counsel of his peers, his regal presence exudes a quiet strength and authority, inspiring confidence and respect among all who gather.

With each elder offering their perspectives on the challenges facing their pod, Kersus remains a steadfast pillar of support, offering words of encouragement and wisdom to guide their deliberations. Together, they discuss strategies for navigating the changing currents of the ocean, addressing threats to their marine ecosystem, and ensuring the well-being of their pod members. Through open dialogue and mutual respect, the council of elders and their leader, Kersus, forge a path forward, united in their commitment to safeguarding the future of their pod and the oceans they call home. Kersus instructs the elders to gather all the pod members to hear his decision and announcement about the pod's actions due to the issues they discussed. He will present his proclamation concerning this matter of great importance.

As the afternoon sun casts its golden rays upon the waters of the Caribbean, the dolphins of the pod gather eagerly to hear Kersus's proclamation. Excitement and anticipation ripple through the pod as they await the words of their esteemed leader, their sleek bodies gliding gracefully through the crystal-clear waves. With a sense of reverence, they form a tight-knit circle around Kersus, their eyes reflecting curiosity and respect for his wisdom. Kersus begins, "My dear pod-mates, as we navigate the ever-changing currents of our beloved ocean home, I come to you with a message of hope and unity. The tides may be shifting, and the waters may seem uncertain, but together, we possess the power to restore balance and harmony to our marine world."

"In the face of the recent buildup of tiger sharks threatening our pod and feeding grounds, rising temperatures, and altering currents, it is easy to feel overwhelmed. But together, we are strong, for within each of us lies a spark of resilience and determination. Just as we traverse the vast expanses of the ocean with grace and agility, so too can we adapt and overcome the challenges that lie before us." Kersus continues, "I am pleased that our male alliances have begun the task of dispatching the tiger sharks and driving them away from our pod. They have taken the fight to them. Throughout the night, they will honor us with their bravery and determination. Our patrols protecting the perimeters of our pod will expand their efforts to provide a clear path for our pod's safe movement to our new home location, that was recently discovered by our adventurous pod-mate Dolphinea and his new female companion, Marina."

The dolphins listen intently, their hearts stirred by the gravity of his words and the profound sense of purpose they evoke. "We shall begin our short journey to our new location as the sun rises in the morning." He adds. "Now let us discuss another matter of importance. After arriving at our new destination and settling in, we will choose a team of our best for a special journey. These individuals will be known for their agility and speed, so they can easily navigate the currents. Also, these individuals will be renowned for their intelligence and problem-solving skills and can guide each other through the challenges they may encounter during their journey. In recognition of, and with the elder counsel's recommendations, and under the direction of one of our most trusted pod members, Jinn will select this team for a journey to the sacred waters of Bimini. There lies some of the answer and the key to correcting the changing face of our ocean—the shifting patterns that threaten to disrupt the delicate balance we have known for generations."

United by their leader's guidance, the pod emerges from the gathering with a renewed sense of unity and determination, ready to embark on the journey ahead with unwavering resolve. Dolphinea and Marina know they have a long night ahead of them. Luna suggests that Marina stick close to her and Dolphinea's siblings for the night and travel with them to the new island sanctuary in the morning. Dolphinea's task is to gather the remaining members of his alliance and create a clear path for the entire group to follow to the island. Dolphinea understands that there may be intense battles with the tiger sharks for himself, his crew, and the three teams already deployed to fight the other swarms of hungry tiger sharks. They part company as Dolphinea and Taran swim off to join the remaining members of the male alliance.

The tiger shark, a formidable predator prowling the depths with sleek, silent grace, commands a presence that strikes fear into the hearts of even the bravest souls. With its massive, muscular body cloaked in a pattern of dark stripes reminiscent of its namesake, this apex predator exudes an aura of primal power. As it glides through the murky depths, its piercing eyes, like cold orbs of obsidian, survey the realm with a predatory intensity that betrays its insatiable hunger. Every sinew of its streamlined form seems honed for the hunt, from the razor-sharp teeth capable of tearing through flesh and bone to the relentless drive that propels it forward in pursuit of its prey.

When the tiger shark strikes, its ferocity knows no bounds. With lightning speed, it ambushes its unsuspecting victims, unleashing a barrage of savage bites that rend and tear with ruthless efficiency. The water churns with the chaotic frenzy of the attack as the shark's primal instincts take over, driven by an insatiable appetite that demands satisfaction. In the wake of its onslaught, there is only silence broken by the echo of its fading presence—a chilling reminder of the untamed savagery that lurks beneath the waves.

In the tumultuous depths of the ocean, a fierce battle unfolded between the sleek and agile dolphins and the relentless predators of the deep, the tiger sharks. Dolphinea, Taran, Xenios, Nova, and the others' synchronized movements and strategic cunning formed a tight-knit defensive formation as the tiger sharks circled with predatory intent. With clicks and whistles that echoed through the water like a war cry, the dolphins launched their assault, darting in and out with lightning speed to deliver precise blows to their adversaries. The water churned with the chaotic frenzy of the clash, teeth flashing and bodies colliding in a deadly survival dance.

Despite the formidable strength of the tiger sharks, the dolphins fought with unwavering determination, exploiting their superior agility and intelligence to outmaneuver and outwit their foes. With each coordinated strike, the sharks faltered, their once-confident advances thwarted by the relentless onslaught of their nimble adversaries. The seas churned red from the bloody battle. Slowly but surely, the tide of war turned in favor of the dolphins, their resilience and unity proving their greatest weapons. As the last remnants of the defeated sharks slunk away into the depths, the victorious dolphins celebrated their hard-won triumph, their clicks and whistles of victory echoing triumphantly through the oceanic expanse. This scene played out threefold as the other teams led by Sol, Medea, and Cersei triumphed in battle over the tiger shark swarms. Scattered and wounded, the remaining tiger sharks in retreat were driven far to the north and westward against the shores of the Florida coasts.

Exhausted yet triumphant, the teams of dolphins returned from the fierce battle, their sleek bodies bearing the scars of their hard-fought victory. As they swam together in tight formation, their clicks and whistles carried an air of satisfaction and camaraderie, a testament to the bonds forged in the crucible of combat. Though weary from the relentless struggle against the tiger sharks, the dolphins' spirits remained high, buoyed by the knowledge that they had emerged victorious against the odds.

In the moments before dawn, the sky blushed with hues of rose and gold as the first timid rays of sunlight gently caressed the horizon. A soft, ethereal glow suffused the landscape, painting the world in pastel colors, whispering the promise of a new day yet to unfold. As the teams of dolphins approached the shallows where their pod awaited, the victorious dolphins were greeted with joyous clicks and leaps of delight. The waters shimmered with an aura of celebration as the returning heroes were welcomed back into the fold, their bravery and resilience honored by their grateful companions. Together, they swam in harmonious unity, their shared triumph serving as a testament to the indomitable spirit of the dolphin pod. And as they basked in the warmth of their hard-won victory, the dolphins knew that no challenge, no matter how formidable, could ever break the bonds that bound them together as one.

# ❧ CHAPTER SIX ❧

As morning broke over the Caribbean Sea, a breathtaking spectacle unfolded as far as the eye could see. The sun, a radiant orb of golden fire, cast its warm embrace across the waters, painting the horizon in a kaleidoscope of vibrant colors. Word spread throughout the pod about the night's victories, and excitement permeated the air. With purposeful determination, the dolphins began preparing for the journey ahead, each pod member playing a vital role in the communal effort. With their vast experience and wisdom, the elders took the lead, orchestrating the proceedings with a steady hand. Meanwhile, the younger dolphins eagerly gathered in the center of the pod, their playful antics adding a touch of youthful exuberance to the task at hand. Together, the pod members ensured that no detail was overlooked, from mapping out their places in the procession to coordinating their movements with the precision of a well-oiled machine.

Luna called out to her children and gathered Dolphinea's younger siblings for the journey. The other mothers did the same. Everything and everyone were set to go. Kersus gave the order, and the pod began the aquatic journey to their new island sanctuary. Dolphinea, Sol, Taran, and Marina took the lead since Dolphinea and Marina knew the way. With Dolphinea leading the way and Marina close at his side, the pod followed in their wake, entrusting their fate to the remarkable navigation skills of their esteemed leaders. With each twist and turn of the ocean currents, they adapted seamlessly, their movements guided by a deep understanding of the ever-shifting tides. As they journeyed onward, their bond was strengthened by the shared experience of the open sea. Dolphinea and Marina continued to weave their magic, their navigation prowess a beacon of hope in the vast expanse of the ocean. Teams of male dolphin alliances flanked the group on both sides, ensuring the complete safety of the pod. Dolphinea and Marina led their companions closer to their destination with each passing mile.

After approximately four hours, stopping for an occasional rest period and a food break consisting of various small fish, crabs, and shrimp, the group arrived in the calm, pristine waters surrounding their new island home. As Dolphinea had described, they found it the perfect place to call home, with waters teaming with fish and marine life, beautiful and serene coral beds, sea grasses, coves, and inlets. A dolphin's paradise! As the elders of the dolphin pod beheld the sight of the new island, a wave of joy and excitement swept through their ranks.

With wise eyes gleaming with anticipation, they exchanged knowing glances, their hearts swelling with gratitude for this unexpected gift from the ocean. For too long, they had journeyed across seas in search of a sanctuary, a haven where they could rest and replenish their weary spirits. And now, as they gazed upon the lush shores of the newly discovered island, they knew that their prayers had been answered and their hopes for a brighter future had finally been realized. Kersus, their pod leader, was pleased.

Throughout the dolphin pod, a contagious wave of joy and excitement enveloped them, igniting their spirits with an effervescent energy. With playful leaps and exuberant clicks, they danced and pranced among the waters, their sleek bodies carving arcs of celebration through the shimmering waves. Each pod member reveled in the newfound sense of freedom and possibility that the discovery of the island had brought, their hearts brimming with boundless happiness and a profound sense of gratitude for the bountiful blessings of the ocean. They spread out in small groups and by twos, exploring the new waters, coves, and inlets.

Marina and Dolphin chose a small inlet to bask in the sun. They needed to rest and relax before swimming for an extra two hours to reunite with Marina's home pod. Marina said, "Well done, my brave Dolphinea." Dolphinea smiled and replied, "Well done, my strong and vibrant Marina. Our pods will remember this day for generations to come. you will be revered and honored for your beauty and bravery!" He exclaimed. They both laughed and sang out with jubilant clicks and whistles. Even the seagulls above seemed to join in the chorus. Dolphinea and Marina, the tireless navigators of the dolphin pod, found solace and tranquility in the clear, calm waters of the inlet. As the gentle currents caressed their bodies and the soothing sounds of the ocean enveloped them in a serene melody,

Dolphinea, and Marina closed their eyes, basking in the peaceful serenity of the moment. In this tranquil haven, far removed from the hustle and bustle of their oceanic adventures, they found restful healing and renewal, their spirits lifted by the restorative power of the sea. And as they floated side by side in perfect harmony, their bond and companionship grew ever more vital, a testament to the enduring beauty and majesty of the natural world.

In a secluded cove sheltered from the currents of the open ocean, the male members of the dolphin alliance found refuge and respite, their bodies weary and worn from the trials of their recent battles. With gentle clicks and reassuring nudges, they gathered together, forming a tight-knit circle of camaraderie and support. As they submerged beneath the tranquil waters, the soothing embrace of the cove enveloped them, washing away the pain and fatigue of their wounds. With each breath of salty air and each gentle stroke of the currents, they felt their bodies slowly but surely begin to heal, their spirits buoyed by the serenity of the peaceful cove. As they rested in silent communion, the male dolphins found solace in the shared bond of brotherhood, knowing that together they would emerge from their sanctuary stronger and more resilient than before.

In the early afternoon light, the new sanctuary basked in a tranquil splendor, its shores adorned with swaying palms and vibrant foliage that whispered softly in the breeze. As Marina and Dolphinea prepared to embark on their two-hour journey, the air was alive with the gentle hum of anticipation, mingled with the sweet scent of saltwater and blossoms. With a sense of purpose and determination, they glided gracefully into the warm Caribbean waters, their sleek forms slicing through the surface with effortless grace. Around them, the sanctuary seemed to hum with quiet energy, as if the very essence of the ocean itself stirred in anticipation of their departure. As they set out on their journey, guided by the rhythm of the currents and the beat of their hearts, Marina and Dolphinea felt a profound gratitude for the sanctuary that had become their home.

As the dolphin couple reached their destination, Jasper from Dolphinea's previous visit swam out to greet them. "Welcome to both of you, Marina and Dolphinea," Jasper said with a giant dolphin grin. "News has reached us about the night of the shark battles and your alliance's valiant and successful triumph over them." "Our whole dolphin community is grateful to your community, Dolphinea, for thwarting their presence in our waters as well as yours and banishing them. Your alliance has done a great service for all of us," he added. As Jasper, Marina, and Dolphinea swam into the embrace of the waiting pod members, the air buzzed with anticipation and reverence. "Our elders are eager to speak to you two," echoed through the crowd, igniting a sense of honor and importance within the trio. Each stroke through the water was met with cheers and accolades, affirming their significance in the community. As they approached the elders, their hearts swelled with a mixture of curiosity and respect, ready to absorb the wisdom and guidance that awaited them.

The trio swam before the assembly of elders, and Dolphinea and Marina related to them the events from the last few days and nights. They spoke of the tiger sharks and ecological issues that caused the extreme southern migration of the predators. They spoke of the battles fought and won on that fearful night and how their leader, Kersus, decreed the movement of Dolphinea's pod to their new island sanctuary.

The elders, their wise eyes gleaming with pride and satisfaction, expressed profound pleasure at the outcome as they beheld Jasper, Marina, and Dolphinea. With knowing nods and gentle smiles, they extended their unwavering support for Dolphinea's pod, reaffirming their faith in the younger generation's ability to take up the cause when needed so both pods can thrive. Their voices resonated with admiration as they praised the unity and determination displayed by these young pod members, echoing a profound belief in their shared future. With ancient wisdom and steadfast guidance, the elders pledged their continued backing, ensuring that Dolphinea's pod would flourish under their nurturing care. A meeting would be arranged between pod representatives to affirm their solidarity.

Marina and Dolphin respectfully departed from the group of elders and swam to where Marina's mother, Maris, was waiting to embrace her daughter with her nurturing mother's love. Maris swam at the tranquil lagoon's edge, the gentle waves lapping around her. A playful glint danced in her eyes as Marina, her daughter, came near her. Maris's heart swelled with maternal pride as she greeted her daughter with melodious clicks and chirps, their unique language of love. Marina responded kindly, her sleek body arcing gracefully in a joyful dance. Their reunion was a symphony of affection, a testament to the deep bond between mother and daughter.

Maris reached out and touched the pectoral fins of her daughter, Marina, her eyes shimmering affectionately. "I am so glad you are home," she expressed, her voice filled with warmth and relief. "I've heard of your adventure and knew you would be safe with Dolphinea." The words carried a sense of pride and trust. "I'm sure you must be tired. It's getting late, and the sun is setting. Rest tonight, my dear, and Dolphinea," She added, "Stay the night with us. Tomorrow is a new day with new hopes and adventures for both of you. I've heard of the proposals your pod elders, Dolphinea, brought forward and the proclamation from your leader, Kersus. There will be a lot of preparation as the team members are selected."

Maris had a feeling, based on her intuition and whispers among the pod members, that Marina and Dolphinea would be the ones chosen for the journey to Bimini and beyond. She had always known, deep down, that this was her daughter's destiny. Maris believed that Marina was extraordinary and destined for greatness from the moment she was born. When Maris first met Dolphinea, she knew he would play a significant role in Marina's future and, perhaps, his destiny as well.

Nestled among three small, verdant islands in the heart of the Caribbean Sea lies a hidden gem: a picturesque Coral Cove of unparalleled beauty. Surrounded by crystal-clear waters that shimmer like liquid sapphires under the golden sun, this tranquil oasis is a haven for Marina's pod community and the place they call home. Many varieties of marine life share the calm waters. Towering palm trees sway gently in the ocean breeze, their fronds casting dappled shadows upon the pristine sands that fringe the shore. Above, the sky stretches endlessly in hues of calm, peaceful blues merging seamlessly with the horizon in a breathtaking display of natural splendor.

As the gentle waves lap against the shore, Coral Cove reveals its secrets, boasting a vibrant underwater world teeming with life. Coral reefs of every imaginable color carpet the seabed, forming intricate mosaics that serve as a sanctuary for a kaleidoscope of marine creatures. Schools of neon-colored fish dart among the coral formations, their graceful movements a mesmerizing dance beneath the surface. Delicate sea fans sway in the currents, their ethereal beauty rivaling any tropical flower's. Hidden among the nooks and crannies of the reef, shy sea turtles and majestic rays glide silently, adding to the sense of wonder that permeates the cove.

Dotting the perimeter of the Coral Cove are three small islands, each adorned with lush foliage and framed by tranquil lagoons and shallow waters. The islands rise gently from the sea, their rugged cliffs softened by a riot of tropical vegetation that cascades down to meet the water's edge. Mangrove trees line the shores of the lagoons, their twisted roots providing shelter for an array of aquatic life. Herons and egrets wade through the shallows for their next meal, while pelicans glide gracefully overhead, casting their watchful gaze upon the glistening waters below. In the distance, the faint sound of rustling palm leaves mingles with the gentle chorus of waves, creating a symphony of serenity that envelops the entire cove in a tranquil embrace.

As darkness descended upon the world, transforming the landscape into a canvas of shadows and silver moonlight, Marina and Dolphinea retired to a secluded lagoon to sleep for the night. The tranquil, shallow lagoon became a haven of serenity beneath the star-studded sky. The still waters reflected the shimmering tapestry above, mirroring the celestial bodies twinkling in the obsidian expanse. Soft ripples lapped gently against the shoreline, creating a soothing melody that resonated through the night. Fireflies danced in erratic patterns on the shore, their ethereal glow adding to the enchantment of the scene. Amidst the serene symphony of nocturnal creatures, the lagoon exuded a sense of calm that enveloped Marina and Dolphinea, offering a sanctuary from the ocean world beyond its tranquil waters.

Marina and Dolphinea share a moment of intimate connection as they nuzzle against each other in the serene embrace of the gentle waters. With each tender touch, they communicate in a language of love known only to them, their bond forged through shared experiences and unspoken understanding. As they exchange playful chirps and clicks, their affectionate gestures speak volumes, affirming their deep and enduring connection.

In this tranquil sanctuary, Marina and Dolphinea find solace and comfort in each other's presence, their bond stronger than the gentle currents that ebb and flow around them. As their breathing and heartbeats become one, they sleep.

As the night descends over Coral Cove, a celestial spectacle unfolds above, painting the sky with a dazzling array of stars that twinkle like precious jewels against the deep indigo canvas. The tranquility of the cove is palpable, with each ripple on the surface echoing the quiet serenade of the nocturnal symphony. Within their families' embrace, the dolphin pod members find solace and security, their sleek forms silhouetted against the shimmering waters as they glide gracefully beneath the moon's gentle glow.

In the calm embrace of the night, the patrols of the pod maintain their vigilant watch, communicating with one another in soft chirps and whistles that resonate through the stillness. Each sound carries a message of assurance, a reminder that they are not alone in their guardianship of Coral Cove. As they patrol the boundaries of their underwater domain, their unity and cooperation serve as a beacon of strength, ensuring the safety and security of their community amidst the darkness.

As the first light of dawn begins to paint the horizon in hues of pink and gold, the tranquil night gives way to the promise of a new day. The gentle lapping of the waves grows louder, a symphony of anticipation heralding the arrival of dawn. With each passing moment, the veil of darkness recedes, revealing the beauty and wonder of Coral Cove in the soft morning light. As the pod members greet the dawn with joyful chirps and whistles, their spirits are buoyed by the hope and promise of a new beginning.

# ❧ CHAPTER SEVEN ☙

Marina and Dolphinea awaken from their peaceful sleep, feeling refreshed and rejuvenated. The morning air caresses their sleek, glistening bodies. Each breath they take is a symphony of rhythm and anticipation; their playful exhales send shimmering droplets dancing in the golden light. The salty breeze carries whispers of distant adventures, mingling with the fresh scent of seaweed and brine. Seabirds glide gracefully overhead, their melodic calls blending seamlessly with the rhythmic crashing of waves against distant coral formations. A group of dolphins went hunting with some of the younger dolphins who were still in training. Together, they drove a big school of Atlantic yellow-fin tuna into the shallow waters of Coral Cove. The whole pod had breakfast together, feasting on the catch.

After breakfast, Marina and Dolphinea joined Maris and Marina's siblings for a light swim and to discuss the day's journey that the two of them would take to Dolphinea's pod's new home. Maris was excited for them and vowed to join them when time permitted. As they prepared for their journey, Jasper arrived with two older adult dolphins, traveling with them to Dolphinea's home to represent Marina's and Jasper's pod as ambassadors. "Marina, Dolphinea, I'd like you to meet Finn and Bella," Jasper exclaimed with bubbling excitement, his sleek body weaving gracefully between the older dolphins and the attentive young adults. "Finn here is known for his wisdom and Bella for her grace," Jasper continued, his clicks and whistles punctuating the introduction. Marina and Dolphinea exchanged knowing glances, their eyes reflecting recognition and respect for their new companions. "It's an honor to meet you both," Marina chirped, her voice carrying a tone of reverence. "Indeed, welcome, pleased to meet you," Dolphinea added, his greeting resonating with warmth and acceptance.

Accompanied by two other young adult males, Dax and Leros, from Jasper's alliance, the group of seven set out. Led by the venerable Dolphinea, the group embarked on the two-hour swim to his cherished home island. The dolphins moved in unison with each stroke, their streamlined bodies cutting effortlessly through the waters. Along the way, they exchanged playful clicks and chirps, their communication a symphony of harmony and camaraderie echoing through the vast expanse of the sea.

As they approached Dolphinea's island sanctuary, a sense of reverence washed over the group, palpable in the air as they drew nearer to the hallowed shores. Dolphinea's home island, lush and verdant, rose majestically from the ocean depths, a haven of tranquility and serenity. With a sense of pride and belonging, the dolphins swam closer, their hearts filled with anticipation and awe.

As they arrived at their destination, a chorus of cheers, whistles, and clicks rang out from the pod as a welcoming committee swam up to greet them and welcome them into the pod. The younger dolphins swam around them and between them with dances of joy and curiosity at this group of newcomers that Dolphinea and Marina had brought to their community. Several elders swam up to the group, and Dolphinea introduced Finn and Bella as ambassadors from Marina's pod who call Coral Cove their home. Dolphinea explained to the elders that Finn and Bella had an important message for the elders and Kersus, the pod leader.

Ondar, one of the elders Dolphinea recognized from the assembly, spoke, "Welcome to our pod and new home, Finn and Bella. We are pleased to host your visit. I am sure our leader, Kersus, will be happy to hear your message. Join us, and we will meet with him." The elders and ambassadors swam together to a cove where Kersus was waiting. Nestled between two towering outcrops adorned with lush, verdant forests, Kersus had discovered a small cove of tranquil beauty. The emerald canopy of the forests reached outward, forming a protective embrace around the secluded inlet and shielding it from the outside world. Soft, golden sands lined the shore, caressed by the gentle lapping of cerulean waves that meandered into the cove, creating a soothing melody that resonated through the air. Sunlight filtered through the dense foliage above, dappling the water's surface with specks of shimmering light, casting a mesmerizing dance upon the tranquil expanse.

Kersus greeted the group, "Welcome, Finn and Bella. Word has reached me of your journey here with our brave son Dolphinea and your equally brave daughter Marina. We are here in this beautiful sanctuary because of their keen eyes and equally keen sense of navigation." Finn and Bella greeted Kersus with solemn bows of their heads and gentle swishes of their pectorals. Bella spoke, "Great leader, Kersus; it is our honor to be here. We bring a message of support and solidarity for you and your community from our pod leader, Paros, our elders, and our entire pod. We are honored to serve you, and we fully endorse your declaration. Our shared ideals and beliefs align perfectly, and we are committed to supporting you every step of the way."

Upon hearing this news, Kersus begins, "Tell your leader, Paros," his voice carrying the weight of conviction and hope. "I believe that together, our pods possess the strength and resilience to overcome any obstacle that stands in our way. As we navigate the vast expanse of the ocean, we must remember that our unity is our greatest asset. By joining forces, we can harness the power of our collective determination to enact positive change in the sea currents. We can shift the tide toward a brighter future for all marine life. Let us stand together, unwavering in our resolve, and embark on this journey with courage and determination, knowing that together we can make a difference and leave a lasting impact on the world around us." Kersus continues. "Bring our message of support and solidarity to your leader, Paros, and tell him I have also decided on the direction of one of our most trusted pod members and advisors, Jinn, to select special team members of exceptional skills and qualities for a journey to the sacred waters of Bimini. There lies some of the answers and the key to correcting the changing face of our ocean, the shifting patterns that threaten to disrupt the delicate balance we have known for generations. I would be honored if two of your pod's finest young adult members joined the expedition."

Elated and beaming with pride, hope, and respect, Finn and Bella acknowledged the honor bestowed upon their pod. With a chorus of honorable clicks and melodious whistles, the two dolphins departed the serene cove where Kersus, the esteemed leader, resides. After some discussion with the elders of Dolphinea's pod, Finn and Bella met up with the other five members of their entourage. Finn spoke first: "The elders, under the direction of Jinn, have chosen those members from both pods who will be a part of the special team to make the journey to the sacred waters of Bimini and beyond." "They are," Bella added, "Dolphinea and his trusted lifelong friend Sol, Marina, and our pod's very own Jasper." Dolphinea, Marina, and Jasper were excited and honored to be selected.

Dolphinea, Marina, and Jasper couldn't wait to tell Sol and share the news with their families, but they knew there was much work, training, and preparation before they would be ready for the journey and adventure ahead. Finn says this to Marina and Jasper. "I will bring the news of your selections to your families when we return to our pod."

Finn, Bella, and the two young adult males, Dax and Leros, departed and began the swim back to their own pod at Coral Cove. They would eat a small lunch of squid, shrimp, and seaweed along the journey to replenish their energy. As midday arrives at the island paradise, the golden sun reaches its zenith, casting a radiant glow upon the pristine shores and verdant landscapes. The waters glisten under the brilliant light, inviting the playful recreation of the younger dolphins and the gentle sway of palm trees. The air is imbued with a symphony of tropical scents—the sweet fragrance of exotic flowers mingling with the salty tang of the sea breeze.

Dolphinea, Jasper, and Marina find Sol basking in the sun with a small group of male adult dolphins. It's a time for relaxation and rejuvenation as the males immerse themselves in the tranquil beauty of this secluded haven, where time seems to stand still and worries fade away with the ebb and flow of the tide. Dolphinea excitedly says, "Sol, you have been selected to join Marina, Jasper, and me as the team going to Bimini." With this news,

Sol sits straight up in the water out of his midday slumber and spins once on his tail fin, letting out a joyous and gleeful whistle. Sol is pleased and excited. He says, "That's great news, and I'm so pleased that I will be joining you, my dear friend Dolphinea." "It will be like old times. A marvelous adventure!" He exclaimed.

Sol, a trusted friend and companion to Dolphinea, embodies strength and vitality with his muscular frame and sleek, streamlined form. His glistening silver-grey skin blends into his surroundings and allows him to glide effortlessly, sometimes unseen, through water, propelled by the powerful thrusts of his sturdy flukes. Each ripple of muscle beneath his skin speaks of countless hours spent navigating the depths with agility and grace. With a playful glint in his deep, intelligent eyes, Sol exudes confidence and determination, his spirited nature always evident in every leap and twist he takes as he dances through the waves. His loyalty to Dolphinea and the pod is unwavering.

The selection news reaches Luna, Dolphinea's mother, and she is pleased and proud of her son. She knew he would be selected because he comes from a long line of courageous dolphins and has contributed unselfishly to the needs of the pod. His bravery and determination have been proven in battle and in his constant quest for adventure. His contribution to the pod by finding and then bringing the pod to the new island sanctuary proves him worthy of being selected.

Delphin, Dolphinea's father, is also proud of his son and holds bragging rights among the other elderly males in his alliance as he retells stories of his son's bravery and adventures to his elder peers. Each time he tells a tale, he seems to add a little extra, which results in an entertaining diversion for his brother dolphins.

Dolphinea, Marina, Jasper, and Sol gathered eagerly at the secluded cove where Uncle Jinn awaited. They approached their esteemed mentor with a gentle hum of excitement and anticipation, their sleek bodies shimmering in the fading light. Uncle Jinn, wise and revered among the community, greeted them with a warm smile and a twinkle in his intelligent eyes. As they gathered around him, he began the pep talk, his words carrying the weight of experience and guidance. He spoke of the challenges on their journey to Bimini Island, emphasizing the importance of maintaining discipline, teamwork, and unwavering determination. He instilled in them a sense of purpose and resolve with each word, igniting a spark of inspiration within their hearts.

As the pep talk continued into the afternoon, the four dolphins listened intently, their spirits buoyed by Uncle Jinn's words of encouragement. Together, they envisioned the trials and triumphs that awaited them on their epic journey, their hearts filled with a sense of camaraderie and shared purpose. With each passing moment, their bond grew stronger, fortified by their collective determination to overcome any obstacle in their path. As the late afternoon sun illuminated the fading daylight in the sky above, the dolphins emerged from the pep talk with renewed vigor and a sense of unity, ready to embark on their training regimen with unwavering dedication and the guidance of their wise mentor, Uncle Jinn. "Meet me here tomorrow as the sun rises, and we will begin our training," he instructed the group.

Under the shimmering blanket of the night sky, the dolphin pod gathered in a jubilant display of celebration and merriment. Illuminated by the gentle glow of bio-luminescent algae that danced in the water, their sleek bodies twisted and twirled in an intricate ballet of joy. With playful clicks and harmonious whistles, they heralded the beginning of a momentous occasion—the naming of their new island home. Sol leaped high into the air, his muscular form silhouetted against the star-studded sky, as he led the pod in a chorus of spirited calls. Dolphinea and the others joined in with spins, leaps, and somersaults. Everyone was present, including the elders, Ondar, Lyrion, Silva, and the others. The warriors Taran, Cersei, and Medea and their alliances joined in the celebration. Dolphinea's parents, Luna and Delphin, as well as Sol's parents, Delos and Xena, swam nearby them as Jinn, their venerable mentor, presided over the festivities with wisdom and grace, his presence lending a sense of reverence to the occasion. The wise and commanding Kersus looked on with pride in his eyes at the celebration taking place before him. As the night unfolded, tales of the pod's journey to the island and their four chosen heroes future journey intertwined with laughter and song, weaving a tapestry of memories and those to be played out that would forever be etched into the fabric of their shared history.

During the night's festivity, the dolphins collaborated on a name worthy of their newfound sanctuary. Each pod member contributed their thoughts and aspirations, their voices blending in a symphony of unity and determination. As the hours passed and the night grew deeper, a consensus emerged. With unanimous agreement, they bestowed upon their island the name "Lumina Island," a tribute to the radiant beauty illuminating their path and the boundless hope that guided their journey. With the naming ceremony complete, the pod erupted into cheers and applause, their hearts brimming with pride and gratitude for their bond and the promising future that awaited them on their beloved Lumina Island.

As the night's revelry ended and the night's darkness again descended upon the island of Lumina and its surrounding waters, a serene stillness settled over the landscape, punctuated only by the gentle lapping of waves against the shore. The moon cast its silver glow upon the tranquil scene, bathing everything in a soft, ethereal light. Above, the stars twinkled like diamonds strewn across the velvet canvas of the night sky, their brilliance mirrored in the ocean's calm surface. Under the surface, the marine life stirred, their nocturnal activities adding to the mystical ambiance of the island paradise.

In the heart of Lumina Island, the dolphins of the pod found solace and companionship as they nestled together in the sheltered coves. Their sleek forms shimmered in the moonlight as they exchanged tender clicks and playful gestures, reinforcing the bonds of kinship that united them as a family. As the night deepened, their voices mingled with the soothing sounds of the ocean, creating a symphony of tranquility that echoed through the silent night. In this timeless sanctuary, Lumina Island stood as a beacon of hope and harmony, a testament to nature's enduring beauty and the spirit of unity that thrived within its embrace.

In the depths of slumber, Dolphinea found himself immersed in a vivid dream that transported him to a realm of mystery and wonder. In his dream, he swam through the ancient ruins of an underwater civilization, their crumbling structures adorned with intricate carvings and symbols lost to time. As he glided gracefully through the silent corridors, he felt the pull of unseen forces, drawing him deeper into the heart of the submerged city.

Dolphinea encountered swirling vortexes of energy among the ruins, their mesmerizing patterns pulsating with a strange and otherworldly allure. Entranced by their ethereal beauty, he ventured closer, feeling the currents of magic and power coursing through his very being. With each passing moment, he felt a connection to the ancient spirits that lingered within the depths, their whispers echoing through the passages like distant echoes of a forgotten era.

As Dolphinea delved deeper into the dream, he stumbled upon hidden caves veiled in shimmering curtains of iridescent light. These caves emanated a sense of tranquility and ancient wisdom, beckoning him to explore their depths and unlock the secrets they held within. He discovered ancient artifacts and relics within the luminous caverns, each imbued with a mystical energy that spoke of a time long past. As he swam among the treasures of ages gone by, Dolphinea felt a profound sense of awe and reverence for the mysteries of the ocean and the ancient civilizations that once thrived beneath its waves.

# ✎ CHAPTER EIGHT ✎

As the dawn broke, a gentle glow suffused the horizon, casting hues of gold and pink across the tranquil, crystal-blue waters of Lumina Island. The first light of day danced upon the ripples, painting a breathtaking scene of serenity and awakening. Birds chirped melodiously, welcoming the new day as the island emerged from the night's embrace. Dolphinea slowly opened his eyes to find Marina floating next to him, gazing gently into his eyes. He could feel her breathing softly as the water rippled between them. "Good morning, Dolphinea," she lightly chirped. Dolphin cleared his throat quietly and replied with a whisper, "Good morning, Marina. Last night, I had the strangest dream. It was both beautiful and mysterious. Though uncertain of the dream's significance, I can't shake the feeling that it harbored a message about events yet to unfold." Despite grappling with ambiguity, he held onto the conviction that it offered a glimpse into the future, a premonition guiding his path forward.

Marina and Dolphinea returned to the secluded cove where Uncle Jinn, Sol, and Jasper awaited them. As they swam up, Uncle Jinn said, "Let the training begin." The four dolphins lined up before Uncle Jinn as he swam back and forth, looking more like a military drill instructor than a dolphin. However, he appeared radiant and wise, naturally commanding their respect and attention to his words and actions. "In a few days, you will embark on the most important adventure of your lives," he began. "What I will teach you and what you will learn will prepare you for this adventure. Some things I will tell you may seem outrageous and unbelievable, but I will share the truth with you." Uncle Jinn explains, "Normally, you can hold your breath underwater for, on average, eight to ten minutes, but in rare cases, some dolphins with practice may stay underwater for up to fifteen minutes. Unlike other marine mammals, like whales or seals, we dolphins do not typically dive down very deep and therefore don't need to be able to hold our breaths for as long as whales or other deep sea mammals."

Uncle Jinn explains that in his travels, he has been taught by a group of Risso's dolphins how to dive to a depth of one thousand feet and hold his breath for thirty to forty minutes. The four dolphins gasped when hearing this. Uncle Jinn continued. "Atlantic spotted dolphins can dive up to two hundred feet and have been recorded holding their breath for up to ten minutes. The Humpback whales you meet in our area when they migrate with their young can hold their breath for up to an hour; Belugas also typically have dives under ten minutes. Like the four of you, Orcas breathe every few minutes but have longer dives of around ten to twenty minutes." "It's not impossible to learn these skills," he adds.

Dolphinea felt confident he would be able to learn and master these skills. He recalls many times he's pushed himself to dive deeper and hold his breath longer while exploring underwater caves. Uncle Jinn tells the group, "For our first lesson, let us move out of this cove into the channel where the waters are deeper and the currents quicker." On his command, the group swims out into the channel. With a deep understanding of their intelligence and capabilities, Uncle Jinn embarked on teaching them the art of diving to previously unexplored depths. Patient and determined, he began with simple exercises, guiding the dolphins to gradually descend deeper into the ocean while emphasizing the importance of breath control.

As the lesson progressed, they learned the art of diving to two hundred feet and mastering the skill of breath control. Under Uncle Jinn's guidance, the dolphins flourished, their sleek bodies effortlessly gliding through the cerulean depths as they honed their diving techniques. With each session, they grew more adept at navigating deeper and longer in the underwater realm, their movements fluid and precise.

Breaking for lunch and replenishing their energy with a buffet consisting of various marine fish and conch, the four brave students were ready for their next lesson. Uncle Jinn tells the group, "You will encounter stronger currents than you are accustomed to. You must learn the skill of endurance while swimming against currents. I will lead you to an area I have found on the other side of the island where deeper cave openings create whirlpools on the surface as the currents flow through from the east." As the class approaches the area, they discover beneath the surface, hidden from view, the tumultuous forces that shape the underwater landscape. Swirling whirlpools emerge like mysterious vortexes, their powerful currents churning relentlessly. These aquatic whirlpools, often invisible to the naked eye, possess an awe-inspiring strength.

At the ocean's surface, whirlpools manifest as dynamic maelstroms, their spiraling motion visible to all who gaze upon the sea. Fueled by the convergence of conflicting currents or the whims of nature's unpredictable turbulence, these surface whirlpools grow to formidable proportions, creating a spectacle that captivates and intimidates the four dolphins. Without hesitation, Jasper and Sol, followed by Marina and Dolphinea, dove into the churning center of the largest whirlpool. As the four dolphins leaped into the heart of the churning whirlpool, a moment of tense anticipation hung in the air. Their sleek bodies sliced through the tumultuous waters, disappearing into the swirling abyss below. For a fleeting instant, all was silent, the ocean's surface seeming to hold its breath in anticipation of what would come next.

Then, with a sudden surge of energy, the whirlpool erupted into a symphony of movement and sound. The dolphins, undeterred by the chaos around them, demonstrated remarkable agility and grace as they easily navigated the turbulent currents. Their bodies twisted and turned with fluid precision, propelled by a primal instinct and an unwavering trust in their own abilities. Despite the perilous nature of their surroundings, they remained resolute; their collective strength and unity worked against the swirling chaos. As they emerged from the depths, triumphant and unscathed, they carried with them a newfound sense of resilience and an indomitable spirit that spoke to the enduring power of life in the face of adversity.

Uncle Jinn was pleased and impressed by their enthusiasm and collective strength in overcoming the challenges of the first two critical lessons. He was confident that he had chosen the right team. For their next challenge, he wanted to evaluate their echolocation and skills in navigating the often tight and maze-like underwater caves. They must navigate the narrow passages in darkness using their senses and intuition. Uncle Jinn directs his crew to some underwater mountain ranges approximately ten miles further out to sea. The expansive underwater mountain range stretches across the ocean floor, its towering peaks shrouded in mystery and grandeur, reminiscent of an ancient, secret, submerged realm. Hidden cave openings beckon to adventurous explorers, their darkened mouths offering passage into a world shrouded in mystery. As shafts of sunlight filter through the clear blue waters, illuminating the rocky slopes and casting ethereal shadows, the caves reveal themselves as portals to a realm teeming with life and wonder. These caverns, carved over millennia by the relentless force of the ocean currents, offer sanctuary and serve as portals to an underworld teeming with secrets waiting to be uncovered.

With a sense of unity and purpose, the dolphin team navigates the dark, labyrinthine caves with remarkable intuition and echolocation. Their clicks and whistles reverberate off the cavern walls, creating a symphony of sound that guides their path through the inky depths. With each pulse of sound, they paint a mental picture of their surroundings, effortlessly weaving through narrow passages and avoiding obstacles with precision born of years of instinctual knowledge. Their synchronized movements convey a sense of harmony as they glide through the hidden passageways, their keen senses attuned to the subtlest shifts in the underwater landscape.

In this submerged realm, where sight is limited, the dolphins' mastery of echolocation serves as a beacon of light, illuminating the way forward and leading the team from deep in the heart of the mysterious caves to the waiting light of day. "Mission accomplished!" shouts Uncle Jinn. "Well done," he adds. "That concludes today's lessons. Let's head back to Lumina Island for the evening meal." The group headed home to

Lumina Island, exchanging thoughts and opinions with each other about the lessons learned that day. The dolphins moved through the water with graceful synchrony, their sleek bodies cutting through the waves in perfect harmony. Their playful interactions and gentle nudges reflected a profound camaraderie as they swam together, forging an even stronger connection between them.

Once back at the island, they dined with the rest of the pod members on a school of giant barracuda that wandered into the waters of Lumina on their southwestern migration. Due to their large size, there was plenty for everyone to fill their bellies. This ferocious fish is a carnivorous predator but shies away from confrontations with most dolphins and large aquatic mammals. Uncle Jinn shares memories of hunting yellow mouth barracuda in the waters of the Indo-Pacific Oceans, from Madagascar to China and Australia.

As the sun began to set, casting a golden glow over the tranquil waters, there was a palpable sense of satisfaction and accomplishment among the pod. With each member eagerly preparing for the evening's activities, an aura of contentment permeated the air, signaling a successful day of hunting, bonding, and exploration. Dolphinea. Marina. Jasper and Sol decided they would share the same lagoon tonight. Their bonding is becoming complete; they are working, learning, eating, and sleeping together as one well-calibrated team.

While the others were floating in peaceful slumber, Dolphinea's mind was racing, and visions of the dream he had the previous night played out in his thoughts over and over again. He quietly swam out of the lagoon and settled among some seagrass in a shallow inlet. Lying back on the soft bed of seagrass, he felt the gentle caress of its blades against his skin. The cool, slightly damp texture was soothing, a comforting contrast to the warmth of the night air. Above him, the sky stretched out in a vast canvas of darkness, adorned with countless twinkling stars. Each one seemed to hold a story—a secret of the universe waiting to be discovered. He lost himself in the mesmerizing spectacle, feeling like he could reach out and touch the distant celestial bodies.

At that moment, surrounded by the sea's rustle and the stars' silent symphony, the worries and cares of the day melted away. However, he was still puzzled by the dream. "What did it mean?" He thought. At that moment, he felt some movement nearby, and a ripple in the water gently touched his torso. He turned to see Uncle Jinn floating in the grass a few feet away. Uncle Jinn spoke, "My boy, why are you out here alone? What is troubling you?" When Uncle Jinn said this to him, Dolphinea knew that Uncle Jinn already knew the answer to that question. "I had a dream," Dolphinea replied. "Aahh, the dream," Uncle Jinn answered. "Yes, the dream," Uncle Jinn added with a wise and knowing look. "I will tell you what it means," he began. "The ancients have sent you a message in preparation for your journey."

"Long ago, the areas around Bimini and the Bahamas harbored ancient secrets that whispered of a time when the world was young and untamed. Stories passed down through generations spoke of lost civilizations that thrived along their shores, their magnificent cities now swallowed by time's relentless march and the ocean's unforgiving depths. Legends told of mighty empires that vanished without a trace, leaving only cryptic remnants of their once-great achievements."

"Among the tales spun by the elders were whispers of ancient mariners who dared to navigate these perilous waters, guided by the light of stars and the wisdom of their ancestors. These intrepid sailors spoke of mysterious islands that appeared and disappeared with the changing tides, their elusive shores beckoning travelers to realms beyond the realm of mortal understanding. Some claimed to have glimpsed spectral ships gliding through the mist, crewed by ghostly apparitions condemned to wander the eternal depths for all eternity."

"Beneath the waves, whirlpools, and energy vortexes would appear randomly and disappear without a trace. Even whole schools of fish, and even dolphin pods, would disappear, never to return. In the shadowy depths, where the boundaries between past and present blur into obscurity, lie the keys to unlocking the ancient mysteries that have haunted humans and our marine mammal communities since immemorial. But as brave adventurers seek to uncover the secrets of this enigmatic realm, they must tread carefully, for the area guards its secrets fiercely, testing the courage and resolve of those who dare to peer into its dark heart. There are many shipwrecks and ancient structures in ruin beneath the waves."

"In our history are tales of cataclysmic proportions, a forgotten chapter buried beneath the waves of time. Millennia ago, when the world still bore the scars of its tumultuous birth, a great upheaval shook the waters surrounding the island, unleashing a wrathful tempest that devoured all in its path. Legends speak of towering waves that rose like giants from the depths, swallowing ships whole and casting them adrift in a watery grave. During the chaos, the earth trembled, as if writhing in agony beneath the weight of unfathomable forces."

"In the aftermath of this ancient cataclysm, the waters of Bimini bore witness to a landscape transformed, its once-familiar shores now cloaked in mystery and dread. Islands vanished beneath the waves, their verdant jungles swallowed by the abyss, while new landmasses emerged from the depths, their jagged peaks serving as silent sentinels over the watery realm. To this day, the echoes of that fateful day linger in the currents that caress Bimini and the shores of the Bahamas, a reminder of the awesome power that lies dormant beneath the ocean's surface."

"Our legends tell of an ancient civilization that once thrived in the waters surrounding Bimini, possessing a mastery of magic and knowledge beyond the comprehension of modern minds. As stewards of the natural world, these enigmatic beings crafted an artifact of untold power imbued with the elements' essence. The Tidal Heart, hidden in the ocean's depths, was said to serve as a guardian of the currents and weather patterns that shape the very fabric of the globe."

"Guided by ancient prophecies and a deep understanding of the correlation between all things, the ancients placed the magical Tidal Heart strategically, its placement dictating the ebb and flow of the world's oceans and skies. Through their mystical influence, they maintained a delicate balance, ensuring prosperity and harmony for all life on Earth. Yet, as the ages passed and the memory of their civilization faded into myth, the guardianship of this sacred artifact fell into obscurity, leaving the Tidal Heart's secrets to be discovered by those brave enough to delve into the depths of the waters around Bimini and the Bahamas." Uncle Jinn continues, "My brave young nephew, that is why we are sending you and the others on this epic journey. To seek out the location of this mystical artifact to be strategically placed back in its rightful place of origin so that the magical Tidal Heart can once again balance our fragile ecological system."

Uncle Jinn adds, "You will not be alone in this task; my marine alliances and contacts are summoning other sentient beings to join forces in the quest for its retrieval and placement. From majestic whales to agile turtles, creatures of the deep will all heed the call, recognizing the urgency of preserving the delicate balance of the world's currents and weather patterns. With your combined strength and wisdom, this diverse coalition will embark on this noble mission, navigating treacherous waters and facing formidable challenges in our unwavering determination to safeguard the ancient Tidal Heart and restore harmony to the seas."

Uncle Jinn concludes, "The ancients have given you a great gift of insight and extra-sensory perception that will allow you to communicate telepathically with other species, enabling you to form a coalition to meet this most important challenge. Sleep now, Dolphinea, and I will help you develop these skills in the morning, and we will perfect these gifts."

# ❧ CHAPTER NINE ❧

As the first rays of dawn broke through the darkness, morning unfurled its golden tendrils over Lumina Island, casting a soft glow upon the tranquil waters surrounding its shores. The gentle caress of the breeze stirred the emerald foliage that blanketed the island while dew-kissed petals shimmered with iridescent hues, awakening to the promise of a new day. Against the backdrop of the pastel blue sky, birdsong filled the air, a symphony of nature's awakening as the island emerged from the cloak of night, bathed in the ethereal light of dawn.

In the shallow, grassy waters of the inlet, Dolphinea awakened to the melodic serenade of gentle waves lapping against the shore. The crisp, salty breeze carried with it the chorus of seabirds greeting the morning, while the rhythmic rustle of nearby palm fronds whispered secrets of the island's ancient past. With a graceful leap, Dolphinea breached the surface, his sleek form glimmering in the early light, ready to embrace the day's adventures in the tranquil embrace of his aquatic sanctuary. He remembered the stories Uncle Jinn shared with him the night before, and now more than ever, he was ready to face the challenge.

Dolphinea, Marina, Jasper, and Sol met Uncle Jinn at the training cove to begin the day's lessons. "Last night, I placed round stones varying in size but weighing proportional to their size in the depths of the cove," he began. "This morning, you will dive down to them and, working in teams, bring them to the surface. Some have been placed in tight coral spaces or buried under mounds of sand and will not be so easy to remove. Working as a team, your lesson will be to remove the stones from those places and bring them to the surface."

In a display of remarkable coordination and ingenuity, the two teams of two worked tirelessly to bring the stones from the depths of the seafloor up to the shimmering surface of the ocean. With synchronized movements and playful camaraderie, they dove deep into the depths of the cove, each duo taking its turn to grasp a smooth, round stone in their sleek jaws. Effortlessly gliding through the water, they ascended in a graceful ballet, their collective strength propelling them upward until they broke through the surface in a symphony of splashes. With gentle nudges and strategic maneuvers, they guided the stones to the surface, where Uncle Jinn was waiting.

At the conclusion of the lesson, Uncle Jinn instructed the four team members to form a circle with him for a group discussion. Uncle Jinn regaled the eager listeners with the ancient tale of the magical Tidal Heart hidden within the ocean's depths. His voice, rich with the wisdom of generations past, wove a tapestry of mystery and wonder, captivating their imaginations with each word. With eyes alight with excitement, he described the Tidal Heart's mystical powers, how it controlled the global currents and weather, and the prophecy that foretold of its rediscovery. Uncle Jinn's storytelling transported them to a world where legends lived and dreams took flight, igniting a spark of hope in their hearts for the adventure ahead. Marina, Jasper, and Sol could hardly contain their excitement for what was ahead and to be a part of this honorable expedition led by Dolphinea himself.

Marina speaks up and asks, "Why haven't humans found this artifact and explored the ancient waters in Bimini and the Bahamas?" Uncle Jinn answers, "The places we are talking about sit in a vast area of open ocean, and only a relatively small portion of it has been extensively explored. Discovering ancient ruins would require targeted and thorough archaeological expeditions, which may not have been conducted in these specific places. Furthermore, locating the Tidal Heat and ancient ruins can be extremely challenging due to the depth of the ocean, underwater topography, and potential obstructions like coral reefs. Additionally, factors like poor visibility and strong currents can further hinder exploration efforts."

Uncle Jinn continues, "Over time, natural processes such as erosion, sedimentation, and tectonic activity can bury or destroy ancient ruins. This makes it even harder to detect and excavate these hidden sites, especially in a marine environment. Archaeological exploration requires a vast amount of resources, including funding, specialized equipment, and expertise. Another reason, I think, is that this environment is not humans' natural domain, and they are not in tune with the elements like we marine mammals are. Many humans have perished trying to explore these vast oceanic areas, searching for treasures and chasing legends."

Marina nods her head in agreement and understanding. Jasper speaks up and asks, "Why haven't dolphins or other marine mammals retrieved the Tidal Heart all this time?" Uncle Jinn replies to Jasper and the group, "Dolphins and marine mammals have a deep reverence for the mysteries of the ocean, including the enigmatic Tidal Heart said to lie within the waters east of Bimini. While we possess an innate curiosity about our underwater world, our respect for ancient relics prevents us from disturbing these sacred sites."

"Through generations of communal wisdom passed down to us, we've learned to coexist harmoniously with the secrets of the deep, recognizing that some mysteries are meant to be preserved, not unraveled." Uncle Jinn adds, "Moreover, I am uncertain, but the Tidal Heart might emit a subtle energy field or vibrations beyond the sensory perception of dolphins and marine mammals. Although we have exceptional senses such as echolocation and sensitive hearing, the unique properties of the Tidal Heart could remain undetectable. Your training and preparations will enable you to reach the depths and hidden areas where this artifact is located. Once there, I firmly believe that the ancients will reveal the Tidal Heart to all of you." "We have recently witnessed the rapid decline of our environment. Whether humans refer to it as global warming, pollution, solar activity, or any other term, it is our responsibility to safeguard our marine environment for the sake of our future generations. Time is running out, and with the fate of the ocean hanging in the balance, the time is now," he adds. With a synchronized nod of agreement, they acknowledge the wisdom of their ancestors and the words of Uncle Jinn. With a synchronized splash of their tails, the dolphin team reaches a unanimous decision: the Tidal Heart hidden within the depths east of Bimini must be found.

As noon arrives over Lumina Island, the clear blue sky stretches endlessly above, complemented by the rhythmic melody of gentle waves caressing the shores. Under the warm embrace of the tropical sun, Dolphinea, Marina, Jasper, and Sol gather near the island's edge, where a bounty of fish awaits their arrival. Against the backdrop of swaying palm trees and the distant sounds of dolphin conversations, the team enjoys their lunchtime feast.

As Marina gazed out across the shimmering expanse of the ocean, her heart thrummed with excitement at the prospect of the upcoming Bimini adventure. The allure of distant shores and uncharted waters beckoned to her adventurous spirit, igniting a flicker of curiosity deep within her soul. Marina felt the anticipation building; her mind was filled with visions of coral reefs teeming with life and hidden caves waiting to be explored. Yet, in all the anticipation and the thrill of the unknown, her thoughts invariably turned to Dolphinea, her steadfast companion and confidante. In him, she found a kindred spirit and a source of unwavering support and affection. Their bond, forged through countless shared experiences and playful exchanges, is a beacon of light for her in the vast expanse of the ocean.

As they prepare to embark on their latest adventure together, Marina's heart swells with gratitude for their companionship and love, knowing that no matter where their journey leads, they will always be by each other's side. Marina knew that with Dolphinea at her side, there was no challenge too great, no obstacle too daunting. Their bond transcends the boundaries of time and space—a bond forged in the eternal dance of the sea. They will begin their journey tomorrow, and Marina and the others will stop at Coral Cove before traveling north-east to Bimini. She can visit with her mother and siblings while at Coral Cove. Marina is looking forward to seeing them and enjoying the warm embrace of her mother before continuing on their journey.

"Concentrate Dolphinea," Uncle Jinn demands. "Clear your mind of every thought except for the words you want to say subconsciously. Project those words with your mind, and imagine sending those words to my mind. Feel the energy transfer between the two of us. Imagine a ball of energy filled with words, sentences, and phrases that you can control in any direction you wish with your mind. See the recipient respond consciously to these words." "Feel and hear in your mind the response coming back to you; hear in your mind the thoughts of your recipient." Uncle Jinn adds. In a clandestine moment of solitude, Dolphinea, his mind ablaze with urgency, delved into the depths of his telepathic abilities, reaching out to his uncle Jinn across the vast expanse of consciousness.

He summoned the ethereal powers of telepathy to bridge the gap between himself and his venerable uncle, Jinn. With the gentle caress of thought, he painted vivid pictures of his underwater realm, describing the playful dances of sunlight on the ocean floor and the graceful sway of seaweed in the currents. Uncle Jinn heard Dolphinea, not with ears but with the profound resonance of their familial connection, and relayed the images he had received back to Dolphinea.

As Dolphinea delved into the depths of telepathic communication, he discovered an extraordinary gateway to a realm beyond the confines of his physical existence, unlocking a universe brimming with unseen wonders and boundless possibilities. With each thought projected, he felt the barriers of conventional communication dissolve, replaced by a profound sense of connection that transcended the limitations of language. Through telepathy, Dolphinea not only exchanged ideas, words, and emotions with Uncle Jinn but also realized he could forge unseen bonds with beings across the vast expanse of the ocean, unraveling the secrets of the underwater world in profound ways previously unimaginable. Uncle Jinn said. "Now you are ready to lead your team, nephew."

Under the serene canopy of the afternoon sky, Uncle Jinn summoned the four companions to gather around him in a circle, their sleek forms glistening in the warm sunlight. With a sense of solemn determination etched upon his wise countenance, Uncle Jinn conveyed the gravity of their upcoming mission, his voice resonating with authority and conviction. As the four dolphin team members listened intently, their hearts brimming with anticipation, Uncle Jinn outlined the intricate details of their final instructions, his words carrying the weight of their collective purpose. With unwavering clarity, he delineated their roles and responsibilities, instilling in each dolphin a sense of unity and resolve as they prepared to embark on their most crucial undertaking yet.

"Tomorrow, you will embark on your journey to Bimini," he said. "No doubt you will meet others along the way and face threats or predators on your journey there. Defend yourselves, but stay on course." Uncle Jinn continued, "When you arrive at Bimini, you will find three large islands and several smaller ones in the island chain. You will also see that humans inhabit them; you will encounter boats and sailing vessels in the waters, as well as human swimmers and divers. Do not let these things distract you. You will meet Atlantic spotted dolphins who live in the area. They will welcome you; they are known for their human interactions. The local humans call them wild dolphins, but they are no more wild than the four of you are. Your presence in these waters will bring much attention to you from the locals and the human tourists."

"Seek out the local marine mammals in the area. Word has traveled to them about your journey there, so they will expect you. In the shallow grasses of the mangrove swamps, there is a manatee by the name of Magnus. He will be of great service to you with information about the energy vortexes that lie just off the coast of the Bimini Islands. "There are twelve species of shark in the waters around Bimini and the Bahamas," Uncle Jinn adds. "Many of them are harmless; many avoid dolphins, but some of them, like the hammerheads and tiger sharks, can be unpredictable. Be prepared for the unexpected and stay vigilant."

"Here's something important that I haven't told you yet," he said. "When you arrive, you must find a human seafarer known as 'Captain Dan.' Both the local humans and dolphins know him well. Dolphinea must communicate with him telepathically about our mission and its purpose. He'll understand, and his cooperation is essential for our success. Captain Dan and I are dear friends, and we've had many shared experiences that have created an unbreakable bond. You will find his vessel tied up dockside in one of the three larger islands' boat harbors or anchored off one of the smaller islands. Ask the local spotted dolphins, and they will direct you to him. Remember, without him, we cannot complete our mission," Uncle Jinn concludes. "Rest, eat, and sleep well tonight, my brave charges, tomorrow your adventure begins."

The four dolphins swam off to find their private places of refuge as the sun dipped below the horizon, casting hues of orange and pink across the sky. Sol returned to his family's gathering place to spend precious last-minute time with them. During the early evening, Dolphinea and Marina visited Maris, Delphin, and Dolphinea's younger siblings. Jasper found a group of young adult female dolphins that had been admiring him since his arrival. There, he found companionship, much-needed personal care, and emotional support. They danced and sang. With each graceful twist and turn, their hearts danced in unison, weaving a tale of camaraderie and affection.

Under the blanket of a shimmering moonlit sky, Dolphinea and Marina found themselves drawn to a secluded cove nestled along the vibrant coral reefs. The gentle lapping of the waves against the shore serenaded them as they swam together, their sleek bodies gliding effortlessly through the crystal-clear waters. They ventured into the secluded cove, hidden away from the bustling activity of the open ocean. Dolphinea, with his vibrant silver-blue skin, and Marina, with her soft silver tones, circled each other in a graceful dance, their movements synchronized as if they shared a secret language known only to them.

As darkness enveloped the cove, Dolphinea and Marina found solace in each other's company. They swam together in gentle circles, their hearts beating in rhythm with the gentle lapping of the waves against the shore. With each playful nudge and each tender caress, their bond deepened, transcending the boundaries of their underwater world. Under the shimmering light of the moon, they shared quiet moments of intimacy, basking in the warmth of their connection as the night unfolded around them, weaving a tale of love and serenity in the tranquil embrace of their secluded sanctuary.

The blanket of night draped over the waters of Lumina Island like a heavy velvet cloak, and a profound stillness settled upon the world. The sea, once alive with the playful splashes of dolphins and the gentle caress of waves, now lay silent, shrouded in mystery. Yet, beneath this cloak of obscurity, there lingered an anticipation—a quiet promise of the radiant dawn that awaited on the horizon.

In the depths of the night, the waters mirrored the ink-black sky above, capturing the essence of the universe in its boundless expanse. The only flickers of light were the distant stars, twinkling like precious gems scattered across an endless canvas. In this moment of tranquil solitude, the island seemed suspended in time, a solitary sentinel amid the vastness of the ocean.

But as the night wore on, a subtle transformation began to unfold. A faint glow emerged on the eastern horizon, painting the world's edges with pale pink and soft lilac hues. Slowly, imperceptibly, the darkness began to recede, giving way to the gentle embrace of dawn. As the first rays of sunlight pierced the veil of night, Lumina Island awakened from its slumber, bathed in the golden light of a new day.

# ✀ CHAPTER TEN ✄

The dolphin team gathers eagerly for their morning breakfast, a feast of diverse fish from the depths below. With synchronized precision, they swim in graceful arcs, each member contributing to the collective effort of herding schools of shimmering sardines, succulent mackerel, and tender squid towards their designated feeding area. As the fish dart and weave in a mesmerizing ballet, the dolphins orchestrate their hunt, communicating and coordinating their movements. They revel in the abundance of the sea's bounty, savoring the flavors of their catch as they share the morning meal together. From silvery sardines to succulent squid, the breakfast spread offers a tantalizing array of tastes and textures, fueling the dolphins' boundless energy for the day's journey.

Excitement pulses through the air like a tangible force on Lumina Island as the pod of dolphins, known for their playful antics and deep bonds, joins in a heartfelt farewell to the brave travelers embarking on their journey. Lumina Island becomes a symphony of color and sound, a vibrant tapestry woven from the threads of friendship and shared experiences. The dolphins, ever the guardians of the ocean's secrets and keepers of its ancient wisdom, lend their playful spirit to the farewell festivities, infusing the moment with a sense of magic and wonder. Uncle

Jinn gives the group encouragement, some last-minute details, and advice, and he wishes them a safe journey. As the dolphin travelers embark on their voyage into the unknown, guided by their instincts, navigating by the stars at night and the gentle whispers of the sea by day, they carry the lessons and wisdom they have learned from Uncle Jinn over the last few days.

Dolphinea and the team began the first leg of their journey, a distance of approximately twenty miles to Coral Cove, the home of Marina and Jasper's pod. Dolphinea, the wise and serene leader, guided his companions with grace and determination. Sol, the playful spirit of the group, delighted in performing acrobatic stunts and somersaults. Jasper, the gentle giant with a heart of gold, swam alongside his friends, his steady presence bringing comfort and reassurance. And Marina, the female member of the team and the most curious of them all, delighted in exploring the hidden depths around them, her playful antics drawing laughter and joy from her companions.

As Marina and her companions glided through the waters, her keen eyes caught sight of a massive silhouette gliding gracefully beneath them. It was a whale shark, its majestic form moving with elegant precision through the depths. Entranced by the serene beauty of the gentle giant, Marina's heart swelled with admiration and wonder. The whale shark's spotted pattern shimmered in the sun's rays that penetrated the surface of the water, a mesmerizing spectacle that captivated Marina and her companions, reminding them of the awe-inspiring diversity and grandeur of the ocean's inhabitants. Dolphinea knows that whale sharks are sharks and not whales, and these gentle giants primarily feed on plankton, which includes tiny organisms such as krill, small fish, and jellyfish. They are not a danger to dolphins. Whale sharks like to linger close to the bottom of the ocean, out of harm's way.

As the four dolphins, Marina, Dolphinea, Jasper and Sol arrived at Coral Cove, they are greeted with exuberant clicks and whistles from the pod residents, their friends, and families. With joyful leaps and spins, the welcoming committee of dolphins ushered them into the sheltered cove, their sleek bodies weaving around one another in a lively reunion dance. Marina and her fellow pod member, Jasper, exchanged warm greetings with the elder members of the pod.

Marina and Jasper joined their families for the short stay, while Dolphinea and Sol briefed the elders about what they had learned from Uncle Jinn and the details of their quest's purpose. Although word had reached the elders about the magical Tidal Heart, there was much they still did not know. The elders were grateful to Dolphinea and Sol for meeting with them.

Saying their goodbyes, fully rested and rejuvenated, the foursome embarked on the extraordinary journey from Marina and Jasper's home waters of Coral Cove to the mystical realm of Bimini, approximately one hundred and twenty miles away. With a shared sense of adventure and excitement, they leaped and frolicked through the waves, their sleek bodies slicing through the crystalline waters like arrows in flight. Guided by the ancient rhythms of the sea and the whispers of the currents, they embarked on their epic voyage, propelled by a sense of curiosity and wonder that stirred deep within their hearts.

Their course led them into wide, open waters, sometimes serene and sometimes turbulent. Through the sun-drenched days and the moonlit nights, the dolphins pressed onward, their bond growing stronger with each passing mile. Along the way, they encountered a myriad of marine wonders, from schools of shimmering fish and southward-migrating whale pods to majestic sea turtles gliding gracefully through the water. The team also encountered various shark groups that, when sighting the dolphin adventurers, scattered in different directions, avoiding close-range contact.

In some places, they witnessed the decline of coral beds and shelves. Where once vibrant coral reefs teemed with life, this ethereal landscape has become a haunting graveyard as coral colonies wither and die under the relentless assault of environmental changes. Rising sea temperatures and ocean acidification have transformed these once-thriving ecosystems into desolate wastelands, leaving behind the skeletal remains of what was once a diverse and colorful marine habitat. As the coral succumbs to these detrimental forces, the intricate balance of life in these underwater realms hangs in peril. Saddened by recent discoveries, the team reaffirms their commitment to restoring the environment. As they swam together, they shared tales of their past adventures and dreams of the mysteries that awaited them in the fabled waters of Bimini, their hearts filled with anticipation for the unknown.

Journeying onward and getting closer to their destination, the companions encountered breathtaking scenes of natural beauty, from towering kelp forests to shimmering coral reefs teeming with life. Finally, after several days and nights of travel, they reached the legendary waters of Bimini. Dolphinea, Marina, Jasper, and Sol arrived at the shores of Bimini, their sleek forms cutting through the darkness like shadows in the moonlit sea. As they breached the surface, the gentle lapping of the waves against the shore welcomed them to their destination, their hearts swelling with anticipation as they beheld the twinkling lights that dotted the coastline.

With Dolphinea leading the way, they ventured into the mystical waters of Bimini under the cover of night, their senses heightened by the mystery and magic that enveloped them. As the team swam through the moonlit depths, they encountered a myriad of wonders lurking beneath the surface—the radiant glow of bio-luminescent plankton illuminating their path, the haunting calls of distant whales echoing through the tranquil waters, and the graceful silhouettes of reef sharks gliding silently through the darkness.

Under the veil of darkness, the dolphin team navigated through the murky depths, seeking refuge within the towering sea grasses and coral outcrops that emerged like ghostly sentinels in the moonlit waters. With their keen senses attuned to the slightest shifts in the currents, they maneuvered with silent precision, weaving through the maze of marine life. Finally, they found sanctuary nestled within the protective embrace of the underwater flora, where shadows danced across the ocean floor and the rhythmic swaying of the sea grasses offered a comforting embrace. Here, in the stillness of the night, they found security, a temporary respite from the perils of the open sea, as they rested and replenished their strength beneath the watchful gaze of the stars above.

Nestled in the cerulean waters of the Bahamas, the Bimini Islands emerge as veritable jewels of the Caribbean, captivating visitors with their pristine beaches, vibrant marine life, and rich cultural tapestry. Renowned for crystalline turquoise waters and powdery white sands, Bimini beckons travelers to its shores, where the rhythm of island life unfolds against a backdrop of breathtaking natural beauty. From the bustling shoreline, where pastel-hued cottages and quaint shops line the waterfront, to the secluded coves and hidden lagoons that dot the coastline, Bimini offers a kaleidoscope of experiences waiting to be discovered.

Beyond idyllic shores, Bimini boasts a wealth of opportunities for adventure and exploration. Human snorkelers and divers are drawn to thriving coral reefs and underwater caves, where colorful fish dart among swaying sea fans and ancient shipwrecks lie shrouded in mystery. Fishermen cast their lines into the deep blue in search of prized game fish, while human nature enthusiasts embark on tours to encounter dolphins, sea turtles, and migratory birds in their natural habitats. With an intoxicating blend of natural wonders and warm hospitality, the Bimini Islands stand as true gems of the Bahamas, inviting travelers to immerse themselves in the magic of this tropical paradise.

Bimini comprises a chain of islands and is the closest point in the Bahamas to the mainland of Florida. It is approximately one hundred and thirty miles west-northwest of Nassau in the Bahamas. Bimini's largest islands include North Bimini, South Bimini, and East Bimini. The smaller islands in the Bimini chain include Gun Cay, North Cat Cay, South Cat Cay, and Ocean Cay. Bimini is home to several landmarks with mystical properties. One of the most famous enigmas is the "Bimini Road," a series of limestone blocks submerged off the coast that some speculate to be the remnants of an ancient civilization or even part of the lost city of Atlantis.

Additionally, the waters of Bimini are said to be home to various other mysteries, including sightings of unusual marine creatures and unexplained phenomena. Local legends speak of encounters with sea monsters resembling giant serpents or unknown marine species lurking in the depths. Furthermore, some claim to have witnessed strange lights or anomalous phenomena beneath the waves, leading to speculation about underwater portals, ancient sacred places, lost cities, or other unexplained activity.

The first inhabitants of Bimini were the Lucayans. The name "Lucayan" is derived from the Taíno word "Lukku-Cairi," which the Lucayans used to refer to themselves, meaning "people of the islands." The name "Bimini" means "two islands" or "the twins" in the Lucayan language. Despite their rich cultural heritage, the Lucayans faced a tragic fate as European colonizers arrived in the Bahamas, bringing diseases, violence, and forced labor. The once-thriving indigenous population dwindled rapidly, decimated by diseases to which they had no immunity and subjected to harsh treatment by the colonizers. Eventually, the Lucayans were completely eradicated from the Bahamas, leaving behind only remnants of their once-vibrant civilization in the archaeological record and the memories of those who came after.

As morning breaks over the islands of Bimini, the first golden rays of sunlight pierce through the wisps of early morning mist, casting a warm, ethereal glow over the tranquil waters that surround the archipelago. The gentle lapping of waves against the shores mingles with the distant calls of seabirds, creating a symphony of serenity that envelops the sleepy island landscape. Palm trees sway lazily in the breeze, their fronds shimmering with dew drops like diamonds scattered upon emerald velvet. As the sky transitions from hues of soft pink and coral to brilliant shades of blue, the islands awaken to a new day, filling the new day with promise and possibility.

Dolphinea, Marina, Jasper, and Sol awaken wrapped in the warm embrace of the sea grass. Rested from their long journey, the foursome ventured out of their grassy sanctuary. They behold the splendor of Bimini's shores, enchanted by the vibrant colors of the coral reefs and the rhythmic dance of palm trees swaying in the gentle breeze. With eyes wide with wonder and sonorous clicks echoing through the tranquil air, they behold the splendor of Bimini's enchanting landscape. The vibrant hues of the coral and the verdant foliage create a surreal tableau, as if painted by the hand of a master artist. Becoming a part of this ethereal beauty, the dolphins navigate with a sense of grace and purpose, their presence imbuing the scene with an otherworldly magic. Bimini reveals itself as a place where the boundaries between reality and dreams blur, inviting them to experience the true essence of paradise.

Dolphinea tells his companions, "I suggest we seek out the local Atlantic spotted dolphins for information regarding Jinn's friend, Captain Dan's whereabouts." Marina says, "That's a great idea." Jasper and Sol both agree. With a flick of their tails, the team set off, their sleek bodies slicing through the water with purposeful determination. Along the way, they exchanged excited chirps and clicks, their communication rich with anticipation and curiosity. As they approached the territory of the spotted dolphins, the atmosphere changed subtly, marked by the unique chatter of their counterparts. The local pod greeted them with friendly clicks and whistles; their curiosity was piqued by the unexpected visitors.

Dolphinea conveyed their quest to the spotted dolphins, his words a blend of sonar and subtle body language. The spotted dolphins listened intently, exchanging glances among themselves before one of them, a wise elder with distinctive markings, offered a broad nod of understanding. With a series of intricate signals, they communicated knowledge of Captain Dan's recent sightings, pointing the way towards his usual haunts along the coastline. Grateful for the assistance of the spotted dolphins, Dolphinea, Marina, Jasper, and Sol eagerly absorb the additional information that Captain Dan's boat is named Blue Horizon. With a series of exchanged clicks and chirps, the spotted dolphins convey the significance of this detail, emphasizing its importance in locating their human friend. The name resonates, igniting a sense of recognition and purpose as they realize they are one step closer to finding Captain Dan.

As they draw near to the shore, navigating the coastlines of Bimini, they can see the outline of small harbors emerging, adorned with clusters of boats and masts that sway rhythmically in the ocean breeze. The sight fills them with a sense of wonder and curiosity as they observe the bustling activity of human civilization against the backdrop of the tranquil island scenery. With each passing harbor, they catch glimpses of vibrant life and colorful vessels, their senses heightened by the mingling scents of saltwater and adventure.

Deciding to enter, they gracefully glide into a small harbor. They navigate through a picturesque scene of fishing boats bobbing gently on the water's surface and sleek sport boats moored along the docks. The air is filled with the mingling scents of saltwater and the distant aroma of freshly caught fish. Humans, both locals and visitors alike, mill about the harbor, their voices carrying across the water as they engage in conversations, repair equipment, or prepare for a day out at sea. Some eagerly watch the dolphins' approach, their faces lighting up with delight as these majestic creatures enter the heart of the bustling harbor, creating a moment of serene beauty amid the vibrant activity of human maritime life.

Despite their diligent search, they could not locate the boat named Blue Horizon among the myriad of docks and slips in the harbor. They scanned the area with their keen eyes, diving beneath the surface to investigate the underwater structures and peer into the depths, but to no avail. The absence of the vessel left them puzzled and concerned. as they continued to scour the harbor in hopes of uncovering any clue to the Blue Horizon's whereabouts. Despite not locating the boat in port, their determination remained steadfast. They continued their search in and around the open waters surrounding the islands.

# ✎ CHAPTER ELEVEN ✎

Captain Dan is truly impressive, as he stands tall against the stunning backdrop of the crystal-clear Caribbean waters and the vibrant shores of Bimini. His weathered face bears the lines of a life spent beneath the sun and salt spray, a testament to his years of exploration and adventure in these magical waters. His deep-set eyes, the color of the ocean at twilight, reflect the wisdom and experience gained from countless journeys above and below the waves.

Standing tall and sturdy, Captain Dan exudes an aura of confidence and competence. His muscular frame speaks of hours spent navigating the tumultuous seas and diving into the depths of the unknown. Every movement is purposeful and sure, a reflection of his mastery of the maritime world. His attire is both practical and stylish, a blend of nautical flair and tropical sensibility. A weather-beaten captain's hat sits atop his head, its brim shading his face from the relentless Caribbean sun.

Captain Dan's voice carries the unmistakable cadence of a seasoned tour guide, rich with the lilt of the islands and the rhythm of the sea. Whether he's regaling his guests with tales of pirate lore or pointing out the hidden wonders of the underwater world, his words are infused with passion and enthusiasm, igniting a sense of wonder in all who listen. Despite the rugged exterior, there's a warmth and approach-ability to Captain Dan that instantly puts his guests at ease. His easy smile and infectious enthusiasm for the underwater world make him not just a guide but a trusted companion on their journey into the depths.

But perhaps most striking of all is the twinkle in Captain Dan's eyes—a spark of adventure that burns as bright as the Caribbean sun. It's a glint that speaks of a life lived on the edge of possibility, where every dive is a chance to uncover buried treasure and every journey is a quest for discovery. With Captain Dan at the helm, the waters of the Caribbean and the shores of Bimini become not just a destination but a gateway to adventure unlike any other.

As Dolphinea and his companions glided gracefully through the crystalline waters off the coast of Bimini's islands, their keen eyes caught sight of Captain Dan's boat, the Blue Horizon, gently navigating along the shoreline. Dolphinea alerted his fellow dolphins to the familiar vessel, their sleek forms darting eagerly in its direction. As they drew closer, the dolphins swam in perfect harmony with the rhythmic motion of the boat, a synchronized dance of sea and sky.

Under the warm Caribbean sun, the sight of Captain Dan's boat, the Blue Horizon, filled Dolphinea and his companions with a sense of excitement and anticipation. Swimming alongside the Blue Horizon, Dolphinea, Marina, Jasper, and

Sol tried to get the attention of its captain. They jumped, darted, and raced alongside, keeping pace with the vessel. They even let out loud whistles and clicks in an attempt to draw the attention of the captain. Dolphinea pushed his mental limits, sending out telepathic messages to the boat.

As the turquoise waters of the Caribbean shimmered under the midday sun, Captain Dan found himself drawn to a group of four dolphins gliding gracefully alongside his boat. Among them, Dolphinea, a male dolphin with a shimmering coat of silver and blue, exuded a distinct aura of intelligence and curiosity. Locking eyes with Captain Dan, Dolphinea emitted a series of clicks and whistles, his communication transcending the barriers of language. Through some mysterious telepathic connection, Captain Dan felt a deep resonance with Dolphinea's message, as if they were sharing thoughts and emotions without uttering a single word.

In this silent exchange, Captain Dan sensed Dolphinea's invitation to join the four dolphins in their underwater world, a realm of boundless beauty and untold wonders. Captain Dan set out an anchor and prepared to enter the water. With a knowing smile, Captain Dan dove into the crystal-clear depths, feeling the gentle caress of the ocean embrace him as he embarked on an extraordinary journey of communion with these magnificent creatures. Through their telepathic connection, Captain Dan and Dolphinea forged a bond that transcended the boundaries of species, united in their shared love for the sea and its secrets.

As the gentle waves rocked his boat above them, Captain Dan felt a subtle shift in the energy around him, signaling Dolphinea's intent to communicate on a deeper level. With a focused gaze, Dolphinea projected his thoughts into Captain Dan's mind, conveying a profound sense of purpose and determination. Dolphinea told Captain Dan through telepathy that Uncle Jinn sent him and his companions to find Captain Dan and enlist his services on an important quest. Captain Dan remembered his close friend Jinn and knew that this encounter was not a coincidence; something exciting was in the wind and under the waves whenever Jinn was involved. He never quite understood the telepathic connection he had with Jinn but also never questioned it. He felt intrigued and very interested in what this dolphin was about to tell him.

In a voice that resonated with wisdom beyond his years, Dolphinea spoke of his quest to uncover the lost artifact from the ocean depths, a relic of a forgotten civilization that held the key to unlocking ancient mysteries. He spoke of the Tidal Heart and the need to retrieve it and place it in its original location to reverse the deterioration of the underwater currents and their worsening impact on the marine environment.

Through their telepathic connection, Captain Dan understood the magnitude of Dolphinea's mission and felt a surge of excitement course through him. Together, they would embark on a daring adventure, navigating the hidden currents and perilous depths of the underwater world in search of clues that would lead them to their elusive prize. With Dolphinea as his guide and the other three dolphin companions, Captain Dan knew that no challenge was too great, no obstacle too daunting, as they pursued their shared destiny beneath the waves.

Marina watched as Dolphinea interacted with Captain Dan. Jasper and Sol maintained a cautious distance because this was the first time they had been close to a human underwater. Adorned with a snorkel and fins, Captain Dan appeared like a curious visitor in their aqueous realm. Captain Dan, undeterred, met their gaze with a sense of camaraderie. He had encountered and swam with dolphins underwater on many occasions. Agreeing to meet with the foursome later in the day, Captain Dan boarded the Blue Horizon. Weighed anchor and headed for Royal Marina for fuel and supplies. Royal Marina is the first marina as you enter from the channel into Bimini Harbor. Nestled in historic Alice Town. He often ties up the Blue Horizon there.

As the sun's golden rays danced upon the tranquil, crystal-clear waters, the dolphin foursome embarked on their journey to the mangroves nestled on the southern tip of North Bimini Island, which Uncle Jinn told them was the abode of the legendary manatee Magnus. As they drew closer to their destination, the air became thick with the scent of salt and adventure. The mangroves emerged like emerald sentinels, their twisted roots reaching out to embrace the shimmering waters. With a sense of reverence, the dolphin foursome ventured into the mangrove channels, their sleek bodies gliding effortlessly through the maze of foliage. Among the tangled branches, whispers of ancient secrets seemed to linger, heightening their anticipation. At last, they arrived at a secluded alcove, where a gentle current revealed the silhouette of a majestic manatee, its peaceful demeanor exuding a sense of tranquility that washed over the dolphins like a soothing tide.

In the serene presence of the revered manatee Magnus, Dolphinea, guided by a sense of purpose, relayed the urgent message from Uncle Jinn to the wise aquatic sage. He conveyed the plea for assistance, seeking the manatee's wisdom and guidance in uncovering vital information and coordinates for the energy vortexes scattered throughout the region. As the words danced through the tranquil waters, a profound understanding seemed to pass between them, bridging the gap between dolphin and manatee. Dolphinea found solace in the assurance that, with this information, they would unlock the secrets of the sea and safeguard its delicate balance for generations to come.

In a moment of serene contemplation, Magnus, the wise guardian of the mangroves, gracefully imparted the knowledge sought by Dolphinea and his companions. With a gentle flick of its massive tail and a reverberating hum, the manatee revealed the precise locations where the elusive energy vortexes could be found, each one a nexus of power hidden within the depths of the ocean. Magnus conveyed not only the coordinates but also a profound understanding of the significance these vortexes held for the delicate balance of their marine world.

In a low, steady voice that echoed with the weight of centuries of wisdom, Magnus began to disclose the secrets hidden beneath the pastel blue waters. With deliberate precision, Magus described a remarkable phenomenon that lay just beneath the surface off the North Bimini coast in the Bahamas—a structure resembling an ancient cobbled road, veiled by the mysteries of time. The dolphins listened intently as Magus instructed them to follow this enigmatic road, venturing deeper into the abyss until it vanished beneath layers of sand and silt on the shelf below.

Undeterred by the unknown, Magus urged them to turn east and continue in a slightly southeasterly direction, past the northernmost tip of Bimini Island, their navigational skills guiding them through the unfathomable depths of the ocean for another eighty nautical miles to the waters of the Berry Island chain. Just past the straights between Ambergris Cay and North Fanny Cay, they would find an underwater cave entrance in the center of a three-mile square shelf at a depth of two hundred and fifty feet in the area just southeast of the straights.

With each word Magnus spoke, a sense of awe and determination swelled within the hearts of Dolphinea and his companions. Magnus continued; "Hidden within this cave is a chamber that holds and protects the magical Tidal Heart you seek. Your journey will not be easy because the Tidal Heart is well protected and preserved. You will face surface and underwater whirlpools, jagged coral outcrops, and ancient ruins that are unstable and reeling in the energy currents that surround the area. Legends and stories have been told that this enigmatic artifact is said to possess ancient powers beyond mortal comprehension and is rumored to be guarded by unseen forces lurking in the watery depths."

"Tales whispered among marine elders and sailors alike speak of ethereal protectors, spirits bound to the Tidal Heart, who ward off any who dare approach with malevolent intent. But it is not only spectral defenders that deter the curious; fearsome sea beasts, their monstrous forms obscured by the darkness, are said to patrol the waters surrounding the Tidal Heart, ready to unleash their fury upon any intruders."

As the words "spectral" and "sea beasts" echo through the mangroves, a palpable sense of fear and apprehension washes over the four members of the team, sending shivers down their spines and causing their dorsal fins to bristle. In that fleeting moment, their minds conjure images of ethereal guardians and monstrous creatures lurking in the depths, heightening their senses to the unseen dangers that may lie ahead. Yet, despite the tremors of uncertainty, the team steeled themselves for the impending journey into the unknown, driven by the promise of uncovering the mysteries that await beneath the waves.

Magnus explains that the Tidal Heart, which regulates global ocean currents and atmospheric patterns, has stopped functioning. This ancient artifact has been inactive for a long time. As a result, the tides and currents have been growing more and more erratic. Over the centuries, it became dislodged from its original location and carried by the currents westward, hiding it within the underwater caves. Its energy source has been unable to control the ocean currents' ebb and flow.

Recently, increasing human activities like pollution and runoff have been adversely affecting the Gulf Stream and northern sea currents. Magnus gave instructions to the four brave explorers to retrieve the Tidal Heart from a cave and bring it to the surface. The Tidal Heart needs to be transported to an ancient site on the ocean floor, which is located ninety-five nautical miles further east. Navigating south-southeast, the explorers will pass through Nassau and continue southeast until they reach the island of Eleuthera. As the team continues their journey through the deeper waters of the abyss, they will come across ancient ruins and a sacred underwater sanctuary. This can be found just northwest of Powell Point, at a depth of seven hundred and fifty feet, on the shelf line, right before it drops into the deeper waters of the great abyss towards the west. This is the place where the currents converge in a swirling dance of energy and life. The explorers have to return the Tidal Heart to its place of origin upon the remnants of an ancient throne. By doing so, the Tidal Heart's full powers will be restored.

Thanking the venerable and wise Magnus, Dolphinea, Marina, Jasper, and Sol, depart the shallow and murky waters of the mangrove forest. Above them, they spot a black-capped petrel rising from the mangroves and flying above them. Intrigued, the bird circles them briefly before veering off in a southwesterly direction, seemingly bound for their familiar home waters. Perplexed by this unusual behavior, the dolphins exchange puzzled glances, their curiosity piqued by the unexpected encounter, pondering the significance of the bird's departure from its typical flight path.

Dolphinea and his companions come across multiple groups of lemon sharks that are native to the mangroves of the northern island. These sharks are social creatures and usually form groups, showing their preference for company over solitude. During the day, it's common to spot them resting on the seabed in shallow water. Lemon sharks are mostly nocturnal feeders, and there is evidence of them hunting in packs.

They tend to catch their prey by approaching at full speed and then breaking once they have the fish in their mouth. Their unique yellowish skin is a master of disguise, helping them hide in sandy waters. Although they can grow quite large, they pose no threat to the four dolphins. They are usually more aggressive as a pack when there is the scent of blood in the water. Jasper and Sol still use caution, protecting Dolphinea and Marina from a surprise lunge from any of the group of lemon sharks by flanking their two dolphin companions.

Upon arriving at Bimini Bay, the team entered the channel and swam to Royal Marina, where Captain Dan and the Blue Horizon moored. The water was shallow, with just enough space to prevent the boat's hull from touching the marina's bottom. Captain Dan recognized the familiar foursome and offered a hand to the water as Dolphinea gently glided past the boat's starboard side. Dolphinea gracefully reached out and made contact with Captain Dan's outstretched hand, their connection bridging the gap between the human and marine worlds. In that brief touch, an unspoken understanding passed between them, affirming their bond forged earlier in the day.

Moored at the tranquil harbor, the Blue Horizon basks in the golden sunlight, its sleek silhouette standing tall against the backdrop of gently swaying masts and bobbing boats. As seagulls glide overhead, Captain Dan bustles about, preparing the vessel for its upcoming voyage. From the dock, provisions are ferried aboard, including crates of fresh produce, barrels of clean water, and bundles of sturdy rope, ensuring that the Blue Horizon will be amply stocked for the journey ahead. Dockside, a fuel tanker pumps golden diesel into the boat's tanks, replenishing its reservoirs and preparing the inboard engine for the challenges of the open sea.

On deck, Captain Dan and his First Mate Milo work in harmony, polishing the gleaming wooden surfaces, tightening the rigging, and inspecting the sails with meticulous care. They fill up the air tanks and store them for the dives ahead. They check their regulators and equipment and stow away their wetsuits and dive accessories. Each of them plays their part with practiced efficiency; their movements are synchronized like a well-oiled machine. As the sun begins its descent towards the horizon, casting a warm glow over the harbor, the Blue Horizon stands poised and ready, its bow pointed towards the open mouth of Royal Marina and the vast expanse of the ocean. With its stores replenished and its tanks refueled, the sailboat eagerly anticipates the adventures that await, eager to embark on its voyage into the unknown.

# ॐ CHAPTER TWELVE ॐ

As the daylight fades into the evening at Royal Marina, the ambiance transforms into a scene of quiet enchantment. The warm glow emitted by the lanterns adorning the shops and eateries along the boardwalk and streets of Alice Town casts a serene reflection upon the tranquil waters of the marina. In this picturesque setting, companions Dolphinea, Marina, Jasper, and Sol opt to stay near Captain Dan's boat, drawn by the allure of the bustling marine life that thrives beneath the surface.

Against the backdrop of the softly illuminated marina, Dolphinea, Marina, Jasper, and Sol indulge in a simple yet delightful dining experience. With schools of sardines and the occasional Bonita gracefully navigating through the dock posts and boats, they find themselves surrounded by an abundance of food. Remaining close to Captain Dan's boat not only offers them a sense of security but also provides a front-row seat to the captivating spectacle of marine life and human activity on shore, fostering a deeper connection to the tranquil rhythms of Alice Town and the marina as they share in this enchanting evening together.

Captain Dan returns to the Blue Horizon, which doubles as his seagoing touring business and home. He notices his new companions floating gently in the water beside his boat and tips his hat to them as he enters the cabin opening to the lower deck compartment. A few minutes later, the inside cabin lights dimmed and went out as Captain Dan turned in for the night. The dolphins do the same and find sleeping places between the pilings and under the boardwalk.

Just before dawn, as the sun touches the horizon in the east, Dolphinea awakens to find Marina nuzzled against him. He gently nudges her as she opens her eyes, glancing peacefully into Dolphinea's. Moments like this convince him how lucky a dolphin he truly is. Jasper awakens and rolls over, exposing his white underbelly as he floats motionless in the water, reveling in the gentle sounds of the marina waking up. Sol, ever playful, wakes up and, with a head nod or two, claps his beak and teeth together in a snapping motion and lets out a guttural click, announcing his presence to all that can hear.

As the four dolphin explorers emerge from their resting places, Captain Dan is on the deck of the Blue Horizon and moves to the stern platform on the boat's transom so he can be closer to the water as Dolphinea approaches. At the stern of the boat, with the salty breeze and the rhythmic lull of the waves beneath them, Captain Dan and Dolphinea engage in their silent dialogue. Their connection transcends mere words; as thoughts flow effortlessly between them, Dolphinea imparts the coordinates for their journey to Captain Dan, the essence of Magnus's guidance conveyed through their telepathic link. As Captain Dan absorbs the coordinates, his eyes alight with determination. He will return to the cabin and check the coordinates on his maps and charts, marking each point with a compass and pen, knowing that each point on the map and charts holds the promise of adventure and discovery.

The Blue Horizon has modern navigational equipment; however, it takes Captain Dan's keen seamanship and skills to sail to the coordinates set into the navigational systems. Captain Dan knows that there may be anomalies, magnetic fluctuations, and energy vortexes along the way that could cause the instruments to act erratically, especially in the mysterious waters of the Bahamas. Captain Dan will need to be prepared for the unexpected. With the coordinates mapped and set, he returns topside to the deck of the Blue Horizon.

His first mate, Milo, boards the vessel. A native Bahamian, he embodies the essence of the islands with his warm demeanor and infectious smile. Raised amidst the vibrant culture of the Bahamas, he possesses a deep understanding of the sea and a profound respect for its mysteries. Captain Dan relies on Milo to help with onboard duties, keeping watch while Captain Dan is in the water with diving guests, helping with the equipment on board, and helping to set the sails and rigging while at sea and when arriving at port on the forty-five-foot sailboat. The Blue Horizon is large enough to transport guests on short leisure trips and diving expeditions. Its modified full keel allows for stable, comfortable, extended voyages in open waters. Its seven-foot draft also allows traversing in shallower waters, yet the hull is sleek enough to glide gracefully and swiftly through the waters of the Bahamas and Caribbean.

In the soft hues of early morning, the Blue Horizon casts off its moorings from the familiar embrace of Royal Marina. Seasoned and weathered by the elements, Captain Dan stands at the helm with a quiet resolve, his gaze fixed on the horizon where the promise of the open seas beckons. Beside him stands Milo, his faithful first mate, whose hands move deftly as he readies the sails for the journey ahead. As the Blue Horizon slips gracefully from the marina's grasp, it is flanked on either side by Dolphinea, Marina, Jasper, and Sol, their sleek bodies cutting through the water in perfect harmony with the vessel.

As the sun casts its golden rays upon the shimmering surface, Captain Dan and his companions embark on a voyage filled with anticipation and possibility, their spirits buoyed by the promise of finding and restoring the Tidal Heart that awaits beyond the horizon. Together, they sail forth into the dawn, united in purpose and fueled by the timeless allure of the sea.

About half a mile from the North Bimini Island coast, a road lies underwater at a depth of approximately twenty feet. Some people believe that the road is the remains of an ancient kingdom, while others think it is a natural formation. Some scattered formations in the area look like walls and there are other unknown structures. The locals and tourists know these structures as the Bimini Road and the Bimini Wall, and they are favorites for visiting divers and snorkelers to explore. Captain Dan knows them well and has ferried many visitors to these sites for a day's exploration.

Captain Dan's entourage, consisting of Milo and their dolphin companions, embarks on the first leg of their journey, following the structures in a northeasterly direction. The shallow depths provide a clear view of the Bimini structures, their ancient formations standing out vividly against the backdrop of the ocean floor. Sunlight dances through the water, illuminating the intricate patterns of the submerged ruins and captivating the explorers with their enigmatic beauty. With each passing moment, the entourage feels the weight of history and mystery intertwined in the underwater landscape. The ruins whisper tales of a forgotten civilization, inviting speculation and wonder about the lives of those who once inhabited these submerged corridors.

As they reach the end of the underwater Bimini Road, where it fades into the sandy bottom, the group presses onward, undeterred by the transition from the ancient structures to the expanse of open waters. Navigating past the northern tip of Bimini and heading east, Milo and

Captain Dan unfurl the sails, harnessing the power of the wind to propel them eastward toward their destination. With the sails billowing and the boat slicing through the waves, Dolphinea, Marina, Jasper, and Sol, attuned to Captain Dan's steady hand on the compass and onboard instruments, move to the vessel's bow.

In perfect harmony with the rhythm of the sailboat, the dolphins engage in bow-riding, effortlessly gliding through the water in front of the boat. Their sleek forms carve through the waves gracefully, a testament to their natural affinity for the sea. As the Blue Horizon cuts through the waves, a playful group of spotted dolphins emerges from the depths, drawn by the energy and excitement of the entourage's journey. Darting and swimming around and under the vessel in a spirited display, the spotted dolphins add an unexpected charm to the voyage, their sleek bodies twisting and turning with agility. Intrigued by the entourage's quest, the spotted dolphins offer their blessings for safe passage and success, their playful antics a gesture of support, before they eventually return to the shallows along the shoreline at the tip of North Bimini Island.

Adjusting their course slightly southeast, the entourage of adventurers begins to enter deeper waters and choppier seas. The speed of the Blue Horizon slows a few knots due to its modified full keel, which runs around fifty percent of the hull length. It has a larger wetted surface than any keel type, which means it has a larger water contact area. However, this makes for a more stable and comfortable ride and helps the Blue Horizon weather rougher seas and ocean storms.

As the pace slows, Dolphinea and Marina swim side by side, the rhythmic movement of their tails creating a tranquil cadence in the water. They seize this moment to engage in conversation, their voices mingling with the sound of the waves against the hull of the Blue Horizon. They talk about home, reminiscing about the coral reefs and pastel blue waters they left behind, their families, and the memories that anchor them to their origins. They also discuss the challenges ahead, with the horizon stretching out before them. Still, their bond grows stronger with each stroke, reminding them that together, they can overcome whatever obstacles may come their way.

Dolphinea wistfully reflects on their journey, longing to return to simpler times with Marina. "When we have completed our quest, it will be nice to spend leisure time together like before the sharks came." Marina, echoing the sentiment, eagerly agrees, "Yes. There are so many things I want to do and share with you." Marina says, "There is no one else I want to spend time with." She adds. "It will be good to be home." Dolphinea moves closer to her as they gracefully navigate the stronger currents of the passage between Bimini and the Berry Islands. Their exchange reflects a shared yearning to restore their playful times and the prospect of cherished moments yet to come.

The Blue Horizon slices through the waves with graceful precision, its bow pointing towards the ocean's endless expanse ahead. Jasper and Sol dive beneath the surface, disappearing into the blue depths below. With each powerful stroke of their flippers, they navigate the underwater landscape, their sleek bodies weaving effortlessly through the hidden wonders of the ocean floor. In the watery realm below, Jasper and Sol's exploration unveils a mesmerizing world of diversity and beauty. They glide past towering coral formations as schools of tropical fish dart among the intricate nooks and crannies of the coral beds while rays of sunlight pierce through the water, casting a shimmering light upon the sandy topography below.

As Jasper and Sol gracefully navigate the ocean's depths, a peculiar sensation interrupts their exploration. A subtle vibration emanating from the ocean floor begins to ripple through the water, gradually intensifying with each passing moment. The dolphins, usually adept at maintaining their equilibrium and balance, find themselves momentarily disoriented by the unfamiliar energy coursing through the surrounding waters. This sensation is unlike anything they have encountered before; its potency is foreign and unsettling to their senses. With a sense of cautious curiosity, Jasper and Sol exchange puzzled glances, their innate instincts urging them to rush to the surface, distancing themselves from the source of this mysterious disturbance with heightened vigilance.

Upon breaching the surface, they are met by Dolphinea and Marina just as the vibrating pulses of energy engulf the quartet, causing the waters to churn violently around them. With each pulse, the surface ripples with an otherworldly force, creating a tumultuous whirlpool that threatens to engulf them. Despite the chaos, Dolphinea and Marina lock eyes with Jasper and Sol, their expressions a mix of determination and concern. Together, they cling to each other, drawing strength from their unity as they brace against the powerful currents and the energy pulsating around them.

With each passing moment, the intensity of the vibrations increases, amplifying the sense of urgency and anticipation among the four friends. They recall the lessons they learned from Uncle Jinn and begin to swim in a circular motion, first becoming one with the underwater tempest and then gradually separating themselves from the outer wall of the whirlpool, emerging in calmer currents.

Aboard the Blue Horizon, Captain Dan and Milo stand firm at the helm, their faces etched with determination as they brace for the impact of the surging energy pulse. As each second unfolds, the strength of the energy increases, causing the waters around the vessel to churn tumultuously. The once calm sea transforms into a roiling storm as the Blue Horizon finds itself trapped in the clutches of a powerful whirlpool, its mighty currents threatening to swallow the ship whole. Despite the chaos around them, Captain Dan and Milo stand resolute, with their years of maritime experience guiding their actions as they work together to navigate the treacherous waters ahead.

As the vessel pitched and rolled amidst the swirling currents, Captain Dan and Milo exchanged wordless communication, their movements coordinated with practiced precision. With steady hands, they maneuver the Blue Horizon, fighting against the relentless pull of the whirlpool with all their strength. With each passing moment, the ship strains against the forces of nature, but Captain Dan and Milo refuse to yield, their determination unwavering in the face of adversity. Together, they stand against the chaos, their unwavering resolve driving them forward as they steer the Blue Horizon to safety away from the stormy seas.

Having weathered the tumultuous whirlpool, the human and dolphin explorers find themselves adrift in calmer waters. As Milo meticulously inspects the sails, masts, and booms for any signs of damage, Captain Dan takes charge of securing the loose cargo, his experienced hands swiftly restoring order to the deck and cabin spaces. Meanwhile, Dolphinea, Marina, Sol, and Jasper float alongside the vessel, their bodies buoyed by the gentle currents as they replenish their depleted energy reserves. The ordeal has left them exhausted but unbowed, their spirits buoyed by the resilience of their camaraderie and the knowledge that they have overcome a formidable challenge together.

Dolphinea and Captain Dan convene at the stern platform, their connection transcending verbal communication as they engage in a silent dialogue through telepathy and human-to-dolphin gestures. With a shared understanding of the ordeal they've just endured, they exchange reassurances and nods of determination, acknowledging the unexpected challenges that have thrown them off course. Recognizing the impact of the whirlpool and the mysterious energy burst on their navigation equipment, they resolve to re-calibrate their position and set a new course for the waters of the Berry Islands. Despite the setbacks, their unwavering resolve and mutual trust fuel their determination to continue, united in their quest.

With a sense of purpose and resolve, Dolphinea and Captain Dan set to work. Through a combination of instinct, experience, and ingenuity, they re-calibrate their location. Captain Dan re-calibrates the shipboard navigation equipment, and he plots a new course. Their actions are guided by a collective determination to navigate the challenges ahead. As they set the Blue Horizon back on course for the Berry Islands, their spirits are buoyed by the knowledge that, together, they possess the strength and resilience to overcome any obstacle that stands in their way.

As the evening descends upon the tranquil waters, casting a warm glow over the horizon, the entourage aboard the Blue Horizon presses onward with unwavering determination. With the fading light of day, their journey transitions into the night, a time of mystery and adventure. As they sail forth, the vast expanse of the ocean stretches out before them, unseen wonders lurking beneath the surface, beckoning to them. Navigating through the deeper waters, they sail over underwater mountain ranges and deep canyons, each wave carrying them closer to their destination: the straits of the Cays.

Captain Dan and Milo take turns at the helm, catching a wink or two of sleep through the night. Dolphinea, Marina, Jasper, and Sol swim together alongside the Blue Horizon; each taking turns navigating and pacing the vessel. As one takes the lead, the others practice a pattern known as catnapping. Swimming alongside each other, their bodies move in perfect synchrony, propelled by the rhythmic currents of the water. Despite the apparent tranquility of their movements, half of their brains sleep. In contrast, the other half stays awake at a low level of alertness to watch for potential predators or obstacles that may threaten the group's safety. As they alternate between periods of active navigation and moments of restful vigilance, a sense of unity pervades their aquatic journey.

# ๑ CHAPTER THIRTEEN ๑

As the first light of dawn casts a golden hue over Lumina Island, the tranquil morning air is disturbed by the graceful silhouette of a black-capped petrel. With wings outstretched, it effortlessly glides through the sky, guided by an innate sense of direction. Its sleek form catches the early sunlight as it maneuvers skillfully, spiraling closer to the island's shores with each elegant turn.

Descending gracefully towards a secluded cove nestled among the rugged cliffs, the black-capped petrel's flight comes to a gentle end. Here, in the tranquil embrace of the light blue waters, awaits the wise dolphin Jinn. Known for his keen insight and deep connection to the ocean rhythms, Jinn watches with knowing eyes as the petrel lands nearby. There is a silent understanding between them. Jinn speaks through a series of clicks. "Welcome, Zephyr, my weary friend. What news do you have for me today?" Jinn asks. "I bring you news about the travelers", he replies through a series of chirps and melodious bird calls. "The dolphin foursome arrived at Bimini Island, and through your local connections there, they located the seafarer Captain Dan." He continues. "Communication took place between your dolphin nephew and the captain."

"The four dolphins swam into the inland waterways and reached the mangroves, where they met Magnus, a wise manatee. Magnus provided them with guidance and motivation, along with the coordinates of the vortex locations. He also told them where they could find the Tidal Heart and where they needed to transport it to reactivate its powerful purpose. Meanwhile, as I flew over the harbor on my flight here, Captain Dan was at Royal Marina, preparing and getting supplies for the journey to the Berry Island Cays and their ultimate destination, Eleuthera Island in the Bahamas." Hearing this news, Jinn replies, "Excellent, my friend, great news!" "Our adventurers are on their way! I will inform Kersus and the elders."

As dawn breaks, casting a golden hue across the horizon, the silhouettes of Fanny Cay and Ambergris Cay emerge in the distance, their shores bathed in the soft light of the early morning sun. The sounds of swift water flowing through the straits mingle with the rhythmic crashing of waves upon the western shores. Overhead, seagulls can be heard calling out as they glide gracefully through the morning sky, their cries adding to the symphony of sounds heralding a new day's beginning. Dolphinea, Marina, Jasper, and Sol, rested and refreshed, swam to the stern of the Blue Horizon, taking up positions at the rear as Captain Dan navigated the straights between the two cays.

As the group exits the swift currents of the strait, Captain Dan begins a sonar scan of the waters from north to south, back and forth in a zigzag pattern within a three-square-mile area. The onboard instruments were calibrated to detect any anomalies on the seabed. The Blue Horizon's depth gauges read approximately one hundred feet deep on the edges to about two hundred and fifty feet at the center of the shelf. Dolphinea. and Sol survey the site underwater using their keen senses and echolocation sonar, much like the Blue Horizon's instruments. Marina and Jasper keep a watchful eye on the depths below and their two companions.

Detecting on the instruments a cluster of hard rock or cave formations among the coral beds that stands out anomalously at the deepest part of the shelf, Captain Dan sets out a buoy marker at the spot, and drops anchor in approximately fifty feet of water closer to the shoreline of Ambergris Cay. In addition, the shipboard scanning sonar detected movement in the same areas as the formations. Possibly a school of fish or something much larger.

Captain Dan prepares for the day's dive, checking tanks, regulators, and diving necessities. Although he is an experienced diver and certified to dive deeper, his depth limit is around one hundred thirty feet without the proper equipment onboard to dive deeper. His regular diving expeditions involve guiding tourists through coral beds in shallow waters. The maximum depth at which a recreational scuba diver can safely dive typically ranges to one hundred and thirty feet without requiring special equipment or additional training. He will remain in the shallow depths close to the Blue Horizon and assist Dolphinea and the other dolphins when they return from the deeper depths.

Dolphinea, Marina, Jasper, and Sol practice the lessons Uncle Jinn taught them. Preparing themselves for the deep dive to the ocean bottom and the caves they will need to explore, the foursome practice holding their breath for extended periods, slowing down their heart rates, and regulating their consciousness. Feeling confident they have mastered these skills, they return to where the Blue Horizon is at anchor.

Close to the shoreline, two green sea turtles gracefully swim together, their sleek forms gliding effortlessly through the pastel blue waters. As they observe the activity around the Blue Horizon, a sense of curiosity flickers in their ancient, wise eyes. They find it peculiar that humans and dolphins seem to cooperate, their movements synchronized as if bound by an unseen pact. The turtles, creatures of instinct honed by millennia of oceanic wisdom, can't help but feel a sense of curiosity tinged with a hint of caution as they watch the unusual spectacle unfold before them.

Sea turtles are one of the most fascinating creatures on the planet. Their species has been around for over one hundred million years and has survived some of the most dramatic events in the history of the Earth. They are known for their large size, unique appearance, and impressive lifespan. Green sea turtles can dive deep; their heart rate slows down significantly, allowing them to conserve energy and oxygen and reach depths of as much as nine hundred feet on average. Sea turtles can live for up to eighty years and spend most of their lives in the ocean, swimming thousands of miles each year. While sea turtles are usually solitary animals, they can often be found in pairs or groups known as aggregations for feeding, mating, and migration purposes.

Captain Dan and Dolphinea converse at the stern, strategizing and formulating a plan to retrieve the Tidal Heart and bring it to the surface so it can safely be carried and stored on board the Blue Horizon for the journey to its original place of power. It was decided that the best course of action was for Dolphinea, Marina, Jasper, and Sol to dive down to the location where the anomalies were detected. Their primary task would be to survey the area visually and search for any possible cave entrance. Furthermore, they are to determine if any obstacles are obstructing the entrance.

Dolphinea and his three companions swim out to the marker buoy and begin their descent into the deeper waters of the shelf. As the dolphins descend deeper into the ocean, the vibrant sunlight starts to wane, casting eerie shadows across the seabed. The once-clear waters have now become murky, obscuring their vision. Suddenly, they notice ominous shapes moving stealthily below them. With growing unease, the dolphins discern the unmistakable silhouettes of, at the least, eight hammerhead sharks patrolling the seafloor. Their sleek bodies glide effortlessly through the shadows, exuding an aura of predatory prowess. Despite the dolphins' agility and intelligence, they feel vulnerable in the face of these large, formidable predators lurking in the depths.

With Dolphinea taking the lead, the team ventured deeper. Along with the hammerhead shadows moving along the seabed, the explorers can make out the remnants of sunken fishing vessels scattered about the seascape. Among the coral beds are the skeletal remains of marine creatures whose fates can only be imagined. Then, at this deep depth, appears a cave entrance; its opening is shrouded in sea kelp and overgrowth. Guarding the entrance are the hammerheads.

As the sunlight continues to fade, the dolphins find themselves surrounded by the menacing presence of the hammerhead sharks. The predators' keen senses detect the intruders in their territory, and they circle closer, their razor-sharp teeth glinting ominously in the dim light. The dolphins exchange nervous clicks and whistles, communicating their apprehensions to one another. With each passing moment, the tension in the water mounts, and as both groups assess the situation, they are poised for any sudden movement. In this precarious underwater standoff, the dolphins must rely on their instincts and agility to navigate the treacherous depths and evade the relentless pursuit of the hammerhead sharks. The four dolphins decide to head to the surface as the hammerheads begin to pace them in pursuit.

Dolphinea, Marina, Jasper, and Sol reach the surface as the hammerheads break off the pursuit and return to the depths. Breaking the surface, they regroup and swim to the stern of the Blue Horizon. Dolphinea excitedly relays to Captain Dan the discoveries on the seabed and the hammerhead shark encounter they had just experienced. "Entering the cave is going to be difficult but not impossible," Dolphinea conveys. "It will require a calculated strategy because of the hammerheads," he adds. "They outnumber us, and we cannot sustain our breath for too long at that depth." After some consideration and translation between Captain Dan, Dolphinea, and the other dolphin team members, Marina suggests, "We can draw them closer to the surface. That will help us replenish our lungs with air." "Great idea!" Dolphinea adds.

Due to their proximity to the Blue Horizon moored just offshore and after observing the unrest in the water, the two green sea turtles approached the group. Jasper and Sol are startled by the massive size of the turtles, but Marina and Dolphinea have encountered and swum beside sea turtles in the past, so they reassure Jasper and Sol that they have nothing to fear from these graceful giants. Communicating with a series of vocalizations and visual clues, the two green sea turtles speak in a language unfamiliar to the group, except for Dolphinea and Captain Dan, who seem to understand the turtles vocally and telepathically.

The male turtle speaks first: "Hello, my name is Varden." The female turtle adds, "My name is Kaia; we have been observing your activities and overhearing your conversations. We would like to offer our assistance." Hearing this, Dolphinea replies, "Thank you; we could sure use your help." Dolphinea explains the Tidal Heart to the two turtles and why they are there. "My dear new friends." Dolphinea's voice resonated with kindness and authority as he addressed Varden and Kaia, his tone laced with urgency. "The Tidal Heart, a relic of immense power, is the lifeblood of our oceanic realm, governing its rhythms and balance. It has been lost to us for eons, and without it, our ocean world languishes in turmoil." The turtles exchanged concerned glances, prompting Dolphinea to continue, "That's why we're here—to retrieve the Tidal Heart and restore equilibrium to our home. However, we face a formidable obstacle: the hammerhead sharks have blockaded the cave entrance, barring our passage."

Varden says, "Fear not. We have faced hammerheads in the past. With our strong shells, powerful beaks, and our skin's ability to absorb nitrogen, we can stay submerged at a deep depth for prolonged periods," he continues. "We will overcome this challenge and help you reclaim the Tidal Heart." Dolphinea accepted their help and explained the conversation to his dolphin companions. Determination flickered in their eyes as they nodded in agreement, ready to face the challenges ahead alongside their esteemed new team members. The new alliance agrees that Varden, Kaia, and Dolphinea will lure the hammerheads to the surface. Jasper, Sol, and Marina will be waiting to execute a surprise assault on the unsuspecting sharks. Milo will stay aboard the Blue Horizon, monitoring the sonar instruments and the surface waters of the shelf. Captain Dan will be in the water, joining the battle with a spear gun and harpoon. With unity and courage, the newly formed alliance prepares to execute their plan and do battle.

With synchronized grace, Varden and Kaia, the two resolute sea turtles, flanked Dolphinea, their stalwart dolphin companion, as they descended deeper into the azure depths where the hammerhead sharks prowled. The water grew colder and darker with each passing fathom, yet their determination remained unyielding. As the ominous silhouettes of the hammerheads came into view, the trio braced themselves for the impending confrontation. Suddenly, the hammerheads spotted their prey and swiftly moved in for the attack, their razor-sharp teeth gleaming menacingly in the dim underwater light.

Reacting with agility and cunning, the trio darted towards the surface with swift strokes of their fins, luring the hammerheads into the waiting battleground above. With a sense of urgency propelling them forward, they led the predators to the surface, where the trio's allies were waiting. As the hammerheads pursued relentlessly, the tension in the oceanic arena reached its zenith, setting the stage for a clash between the two opposing forces. In a frenzied clash on the surface and beneath the waves, the alliance of sea turtles, dolphins, and the human Captain Dan engage in a brutal struggle against the formidable squadron of eight hammerhead sharks, staunch defenders of the entrance to the underwater cave. With their combined strength and ferocity, the intrepid band of aquatic warriors charge headlong into the fray, determined to overcome their adversaries and secure passage to the hidden depths beyond. As the hammerheads close in with predatory precision, teeth bared and fins slicing through the water, the dolphins and sea turtles brace themselves for the imminent confrontation.

With lightning-fast strikes and coordinated maneuvers, Dolphinea, Marina, Jasper, and Sol, and the sea turtles Varden and Kaia launch a relentless assault against the hammerhead sharks, their combined efforts driving the predators back with each successive blow. With his formidable skills with a spear gun, knife, and harpoon gleaming like a beacon of hope amidst the chaos,

Captain Dan delivers decisive strikes, further weakening the resolve of their adversaries. As the battle rages on, the waters become a swirling tempest of blood and fury, but the alliance of dolphins, sea turtles, and humans remains resolute. With a strong, final coordinated push, they force the remaining hammerhead sharks into a hasty retreat, driving them away into the abyss and away from the shelf, securing victory over the entrance to the underwater cave.

As the turbulence of battle fades and the waters of the shelf regain their tranquil serenity, the alliance of dolphins, sea turtles, and humans finds themselves basking in the glow of their hard-earned victory. Though wearied and bearing scars from the harrowing encounter with the hammerhead sharks, a sense of triumph permeates the group as they survey the scene of their hard-fought battle. Each member, be it a dolphin, sea turtle, or human, shares in the satisfaction of overcoming adversity through unity and mutual cooperation.

Amidst the calm waters, the alliance finds solace in the bonds forged amidst the chaos of battle. The dolphins chirp and click in celebration, their playful arcs through the water serving as a testament to their resilience and camaraderie. With their steady presence and ancient wisdom, the sea turtles offer silent nods of acknowledgment, their shells bearing the marks of their brave deeds. And the humans, humbled by the bravery of their aquatic allies, stand in awe of the courage and strength displayed by their fellow creatures of the sea.

As they regroup and tend to their wounds, the alliance reflects on the significance of their triumph. Beyond the defeat of the hammerhead sharks lies a more profound lesson: that in unity, there is strength, and in cooperation, there is victory. And so, amidst the gentle sway of the ocean currents, the dolphin, turtle, and human alliance find renewed purpose and determination, ready to face whatever challenges may lie ahead, secure in the knowledge that together they are an unstoppable force of nature.

# ❧ CHAPTER FOURTEEN ❧

The day's activities stretch into the late afternoon as the shoreline is bathed in the warm, golden hues of the setting sun, casting a serene glow over the tranquil waters and casting a calm aura over the shallow waters where the Blue Horizon and its unique alliance of dolphins, turtles, and humans find sanctuary. With the gentle lapping of the waves against the vessel's hull as their soundtrack, the alliance gathers at the stern of the boat, their weary yet contented faces illuminated by the fading light.

Onboard the Blue Horizon, Captain Dan and Milo recount the day's endeavors and the spectacle they witnessed and participated in. They share tales of exploration and discovery, their laughter, mingling with the gentle rhythm of the ocean waves. In the embrace of the setting sun, the Blue Horizon and its maritime alliance find solace and camaraderie, united by their shared passion for the sea, its wonders, and their quest. The brilliant colors of the sunset gradually fade into the twilight hues, casting a tranquil ambiance across the Berry Islands and the Cays. Along the shoreline of Ambergris Cay, the marine alliance finds sanctuary in the shallow waters, the Blue Horizon gently rocking with the rhythm of the ocean waves. Against the backdrop of the darkening sky, the alliance members settle in for the night, their weary bodies finding solace in the comforting embrace of the sea. With the stars beginning to twinkle overhead and the distant sound of nocturnal creatures echoing through the air under the canopy of the night sky, they sleep and heal.

Morning breaks, ushering in a fresh day. The waters come alive, teeming with schools of fish and sea birds soaring above. The sea companions awaken, rejuvenated, and ready for the day ahead, though hunger gnaws at their stomachs after yesterday's exertions. Varden and Kaia, both herbivores, feast on seagrass, kelp, and algae, while Dolphinea, Marina, Sol, and Jasper indulge in a meal of herring and anchovies. Meanwhile, aboard the Blue Horizon, the aroma of brewing coffee, sizzling bacon, and eggs fills the galley. Satisfying their hunger, the team convenes at the stern platform of the Blue Horizon to plan out their cave expedition and retrieval of the Tidal Heart.

During today's expedition, the team has decided on the following strategy: Varden and Kaia will stand guard outside the cave entrance, while Dolphinea, Marina, Jasper, and Sol will venture inside the cave. They will explore the cave's interior, navigating its underwater corridors and tunnels in search of the Tidal Hearts chamber. When the Tidal Heart is retrieved, they will bring it to the surface, and Captain Dan and Milo will be waiting to get it onboard the Blue Horizon to transport it to its place of origin. With their plan in mind, the alliance of dolphins and turtles slip below the surface and begin their descent toward the cave entrance. As they approach the entrance, the sands in front of the cave are clear of movements or shadows, and no hammerheads are present. Remnants of sunken boats and debris are scattered about, most likely carried here by the currents of the Atlantic and Gulf streams, they assume.

Varden and Kaia position themselves as sentinels outside the cave entrance, while Dolphinea leads Marina, Jasper, and Sol single-file into the mouth of the cave. The four dolphins move with graceful precision as they glide single-file through the darkened passages of the cave, their sleek bodies cutting through the water with ease. Illuminated by the soft glow of bio-luminescent organisms adorning the walls and ceiling, the cave seems to pulse with an otherworldly radiance. Ribbons of light dance across the rocky surfaces, casting intricate patterns that shimmer and fade with each passing moment. Despite the eerie beauty of their surroundings, the dolphins press forward, their mission clear, as they navigate deeper into the heart of the cavern.

As they progress, the walls and passages of the cave come alive with a vibrant luminosity, each twist and turn revealing new wonders to behold. The bio-luminescent display intensifies, bathing the underwater landscape in a kaleidoscope of colors that shift and morph with each dolphin's movements. Yet, amidst the mesmerizing spectacle, a sense of caution hangs heavy in the air as the dolphins approach the open chamber at the cave's rear. Here, standing guard like a silent sentinel, looms an enormous beast, its form obscured by shadows cast by the dim glow emanating from within. With bated breath, the dolphins pause, their instincts warning them of the formidable presence ahead.

In the shadowy recesses of the Bahamian underwater caves, tales tell of an evil presence lurking, known only as the Lusca, an embodiment of terror said to haunt the depths with its sinister aura. Described as an octopus of immense proportions, the Lusca's writhing arms extend like tendrils of darkness, reaching out to ensnare unsuspecting prey that dares to venture too close to its domain. Its bulbous head, adorned with rows of razor-sharp beaks and eyes that glimmer with an unholy light, strikes fear into the hearts of even the most seasoned divers.

Legends speak of the Lusca as a harbinger of doom, its very presence signaling imminent danger to those who dare to cross its path. Some say it feeds on the souls of the lost, dragging unfortunate victims into the abyssal depths from which it emerged, their screams echoing through the cavernous chambers long after they have disappeared. Some say it guards hidden treasures buried within the labyrinthine recesses of the underwater caves. In contrast, others speak of its role as a sentinel, protecting the secrets of the deep from the prying eyes of humanity. Yet, there are darker whispers of wayward divers ensnared by its writhing tentacles, dragged into the caves, never to be seen again. Whether myth or reality, the legend of the Lusca casts a spell of awe and apprehension over those who venture into the silent realms beneath the Bahamian waters.

Hearts pounding, the four companions fall back as the behemoth comes into view. They see looming in front of them a massive octopus, its eyes glowing with an otherworldly luminescence that pierces the darkness of the caverns and its sinewy arms adorned with suckers capable of trapping even the most intrepid explorers. This unexpected encounter sends chills up and down their spines. Gasping and struggling to breathe in the cramped space of the cave, the foursome retreats to the safety of the open water outside the cave. As the dolphins emerge from the cave mouth and launch towards the surface above, Varden and Kaia, the two turtle sentinels, can see and feel the panic in their eyes and actions. Varden and Kaia follow their dolphin companions to the surface.

Once again, the alliance meets at the stern platform of the Blue Horizon. As their heart rates return to normal and the fear and panic recede, Dolphinea conveys to Captain Dan, Varden, and Kaia the encounter with a monstrous octopus unlike anything he has ever seen, whose dark presence looms large within the underwater cave. Captain Dan retells a story passed down by the locals around the islands that is said to have originated with the Lucayan people, the original people of the Bahamas.

The legend of the mystical creature, the Lusca. Tales the islanders tell depict this enigmatic creature as a formidable amalgamation of the sea's most fearsome denizens. Legends intertwine with cautionary tales to warn those who would dare to trespass into the domain of the Lusca to beware the whispers of the Lusca, for to encounter this evil entity in the underwater caves of the Bahamas is to tempt fate itself, risking not only one's life but also one's very soul to the darkness that dwells beneath the waves. Captain Dan believes that what lurks in the cave below is the legendary creature. Hearing this tale causes the group to gasp with a shudder and convinces them that what they are about to battle with is a formidable force requiring drastic measures.

As they recalled their strategy to lure the hammerheads to the surface before battling them the day before, they decided to attempt the same approach: an audacious plan to lure the evil sea beast out of its dark domain within the underwater cave. With cunning strategy and unwavering determination, the alliance of sea turtles and dolphins will orchestrate a daring ambush, using themselves as bait to draw the monstrous octopus out into the open. Moving forward with their plan the dolphin and turtle warriors return to the depths of the cave entrance. Marina, Jasper, Varden, and

Kaia wait outside the cave opening, creating a disturbance in the water. They stay ready for the Lusca to appear, their anticipation palpable in the murky water. Dolphinea and Sol prepare to embark on their daring mission. With hearts pounding with adrenaline and determination, they glide into the darkened depths of the underwater cave, their senses alert for any sign of the lurking Lusca.

Inside the cavern's labyrinthine passages, Dolphinea and Sol move with cautious yet purposeful strides, their movements guided by instinct and strategy. With each echoing click and chirp, they communicate silently, their plan unfolding meticulously. As they navigate the treacherous terrain, they know that their comrades' fate and safety hang in the balance. With unwavering resolve, they press forward, their mission clear: to lure the malevolent Lusca out of hiding and into the open waters where their allies stand, ready to confront the creature head-on. As they round the final corner, they come face-to-face with the ominous silhouette of the Lusca, its massive form poised and ready to strike.

With hearts pounding and adrenaline coursing through their veins, Dolphinea and Sol hold their ground; their unwavering resolve is a beacon of defiance against the darkness that lurks within the depths. In a mesmerizing display of skill and bravery, Dolphinea and Sol execute their plan flawlessly, drawing the Lusca out of its lair and into the open waters where their comrades stand ready to engage in battle. As the creature emerges from the shadows, its malevolent presence casting a shadow over the surrounding seascape, the stage is set for a showdown of epic proportions. Dolphinea and Sol steel themselves for the confrontation ahead as they rejoin their allies.

In a scene from the annals of oceanic folklore, the noble sea turtles join forces with the brave dolphins to confront the dreaded Lusca, the evil guardian of the underwater caves. With a sense of determination as deep as the ocean, the unlikely alliance charges forward, their collective resolve unyielding in the face of the looming threat. With their agility and speed, the dolphins lead the charge, while the sea turtles, with their ancient wisdom and resilient shells, provide a steadfast backbone to the assault.

The underwater arena becomes a symphony of swirling currents and frenetic motion as the battle commences. The dolphins and sea turtles move in perfect harmony, their coordinated attacks striking at the heart of the Lusca's defenses. With each powerful blow, they chip away at the creature's strength. Enraged by the audacity of its adversaries, the Lusca lashes out in all directions with its suction cup, razor sharp tentacles, catching and wrapping one of its massive tentacles around Jasper's body.

Reeling and struggling to hold his breath and break free from the Lusca's grasp, Jasper thrashes about. Blood was oozing from his blowhole and around his torso. Just at that moment, out of the depths came a large male swordfish. Heading directly for the Lusca, the swordfish's pointed, broad bill slashes back and forth in the water as he strikes the evil beast, slicing and dicing through the thick part of the tentacle close to the Lusca's body, ripping it from the torso of the Lusca and from around the torso of the brave dolphin Jasper. As the Lusca pauses its assault and pulls back its remaining tentacles, Jasper floats to the seabed, beaten and battered, his body bleeding and his chest heaving in pain.

Marina comes to Jasper's aid without hesitation and with the speed she is famous for, sliding under him with her belly facing up and her back and dorsal fin against the ocean floor. She cradles Jasper between her pectoral fins and tail fin. Marina swims on her back with Jasper resting in the safety of her upturned underside, lifting him to the surface and the shallow waters where the Blue Horizon is anchored. She stays with him, reassuring him and helping him regain his breath and composure.

Below the surface, in the depths, the battle ensues. The sea turtles and swordfish move with calculated precision; their movements are coordinated perfectly. With the swordfish's razor-sharp bill leading the charge, they launch a series of lightning-fast strikes, aiming for the vulnerable spots beneath the Lusca's underside. Despite the Lusca's formidable strength and cunning, the combined might of the dolphins, sea turtles, and swordfish proves its undoing. In a breathtaking display of courage and unity, the dolphins and sea turtles press their advantage, driving the Lusca back with each successive blow.

They wear down the creature's defenses with relentless determination, exploiting every opening with calculated strikes. With a final coordinated effort, they deliver a decisive blow, incapacitating the Lusca and sending it retreating into the depths of the abyss, leaving a cloudy trail of black ink in its wake as a distraction, obscuring the Lusca from the eyes of its vanquishers and allowing it to slink into the shadows of the abyss. Its reign of terror over the underwater cave was finally ended. With their adversary vanquished and the underwater cave reclaimed, the dolphins, sea turtles, and lone swordfish emerge as true heroes, their bravery etched into the annals of Bahamian legend for generations to come.

Returning to the surface, the alliance members convene in the shallow waters close to shore. Kaia brings strands of seaweed leaves and kelp to wrap Jasper's wounds as a healing salve. She tells the group that this particular variety of kelp is from the Sargasso Sea, brought here by the currents, and is full of healing properties and nutrients. Kaia and Marina also feed Jasper algae, which will help heal his internal wounds and clear his airways. His prognosis for a full recovery is promising, and he should be seaworthy in a day or two. Dolphinea, Marina, and Sol gather around their friend Jasper, relief evident in their expressions as they hear the news of his impending recovery. With gentle words and comforting gestures, they reassure him that he will return to his old self in no time, showering him with praise for his bravery and unwavering devotion to them and their quest. Their voices ring with sincerity as they express gratitude for Jasper's steadfast loyalty, acknowledging the integral role he played in the battle against the Lusca and the ultimate victory they achieved together.

The swordfish that joined forces with the dolphins in their battle against the Lusca emerges from the depths with a majestic and imposing presence. Its sleek body, adorned with shimmering scales of a deep, iridescent blue hue, glints in the sunlight filtering down from the surface above. The swordfish's streamlined form is a testament to its agility and speed, perfectly designed for navigating the ocean currents with grace and precision. At the forefront of its formidable physique is the unmistakable elongated bill, a testament to its namesake and a weapon honed through countless battles beneath the waves. With his eyes that gleam with intelligence and determination, the male swordfish stands ready to lend its formidable strength to the alliance's noble cause.

Dolphinea communicates telepathically in a language understood by the swordfish, showing his deep appreciation for the help he provided in defeating the Lusca and for saving Jasper from the clutches of the beast, thus saving his life. He asks the swordfish his name and if he would join the alliance on their quest. With a dignified demeanor, the male swordfish introduces himself as Nereus, his voice carrying the weight of experience and determination. He affirms his commitment to the cause, expressing his readiness to lend his strength and expertise to their endeavors. Dolphinea nods appreciatively, a sense of gratitude swelling within him as he welcomes Nereus into their alliance, recognizing the invaluable addition his presence will bring to their collective efforts.

# ᢒ CHAPTER FIFTEEN ᢒ

Evening descends upon the aquatic shelf, signaling the end of the day's expedition. The team, eager to retrieve the Tidal Heart from the cave, acknowledges the importance of safety and opts to postpone their retrieval mission until the morning. Rest and recuperation are deemed necessary after the day's exertions, ensuring they are prepared for the task ahead. Having rested submerged in the cave for ages, the Tidal Heart can endure another night without disturbance.

The group dined on a variety of sea delicacies, each to their own tastes and preferences. The wise and compassionate Kaia remains by Jasper's side, monitoring his recovery and administering healing herbs and dressings. Varden and Sol find resting places close by to provide protection or assistance to the others. Marina and Dolphinea float next to each other, their fins touching, creating closeness as their tails sway in unison beneath the surface.

Nereus, the newest member of the alliance, demonstrates impressive agility as he swiftly dives and leaps through the waters surrounding the perimeter of the shelf. With each graceful movement, he hunts for fish, his keen eyes scanning the depths for any sign of prey. Yet, amidst his pursuit of sustenance, Nereus remains vigilant, ever watchful for potential threats lurking beneath the waves. His presence serves as a guardian, ensuring the safety and security of the alliance.

Captain Dan and Milo retire onboard the Blue Horizon for the night, finding solace in the gentle sway of the vessel upon the tranquil waters. The glow of the half-moon casts shimmering beams that dance across the surface, painting the scene with surreal beauty. Above, the stars twinkle in the night sky, creating a mesmerizing spectacle that serves as a soothing backdrop to their restful evening.

Morning arrives, accompanied by the soft glow of dawn spreading across the horizon. The glassy, clear water beckons to the marine and human alliance members, reminding them that today marks the culmination of their efforts—the day they will venture into the cave's inner chamber to recover the Tidal Heart. With anticipation coursing through their veins, they prepare themselves for the task ahead, knowing that success could bring profound change to both worlds.

Dolphinea, Marina, Sol, and Varden will make their way to the cave. Sol and Varden will remain outside, while Dolphinea and Marina will enter the cave, weaving through the corridors and passageways until they reach the inner chamber. Once there, they will retrieve the Tidal Heart from the cave, and the foursome, Dolphinea, Marina,

Sol, and Varden, will bring the Tidal Heart to the surface to be taken on board the Blue Horizon.

The foursome make their descent. When they arrive at the cave entrance, Dolphinea and Marina glide gracefully into the cave, their sleek bodies cutting through the water with ease as together they navigate the narrow corridors and passageways. Reminiscent of their adventures exploring the underwater caves on the day they met, a feeling of closeness, tinged with a sense of adventure and anticipation, filled their senses. The cave's walls and ceiling are adorned with bio-luminescent organisms, casting an ethereal glow that illuminates their path. Each twist and turn reveals new wonders of the cave's natural beauty, with vibrant hues dancing across the rocky surfaces, creating a mesmerizing spectacle that captivates the senses.

As they reach the inner chamber, awe washes over them as they take in the scene before them. The chamber is a realm of magic and mystery, with stalactites and stalagmites towering like ancient sentinels, their surfaces adorned with shimmering crystals that glimmer in the faint light. A gentle hum fills the air, resonating with the energy of the Tidal Heart. The water here seems to pulse with a life of its own, reflecting the glow of the bio-luminescent organisms and creating an otherworldly ambiance that transports the dolphins to a realm beyond imagination. It's a place where reality and fantasy intertwine, a place where the boundaries between the mundane and the mystical blur, leaving the dolphins spellbound by the sheer magnificence of it all.

At the rear of the chamber sits the Tidal Heart, a magnificent sight to behold. Bathed in a magical and mysterious glow, it emanates a mesmerizing illumination of colors. Shades of blues, aquas, and cerulean intertwine, swirling around the heart in a hypnotic dance that captivates the onlookers. Each hue seems to pulsate with its own energy, casting radiant beams of light that illuminate the chamber with an ethereal brilliance.

The Tidal Heart itself appears as if it's alive, its surface shimmering with iridescence as though infused with the very essence of the ocean itself. Waves of energy ripple across its form, creating an aura of power and ancient wisdom that permeates the air. As the dolphins draw nearer, they can feel the pull of its enchantment, beckoning them to unlock its secrets and unleash its potential. It's a scene of unparalleled beauty and mystique, a treasure trove of wonder hidden within the depths of the cave's inner sanctum.

As Dolphinea and Marina cautiously reach out to nudge the Tidal Heart from its resting place, a hush falls over the chamber as its luminance begins to fade. A palpable shift occurs—the luminance fades, and the pulsating energy ceases. Gradually, the vibrant hues of the Tidal Heart begin to diminish, its once radiant colors fading into a soft pastel aqua blue. The chamber is bathed in a serene glow as the heart's aura subsides, leaving an air of tranquility in its wake. It's as if the heart has relinquished its power for the moment, inviting the dolphins to contemplate the significance of their discovery amidst the calm that now envelops them.

Marina and Dolphinea share a moment of understanding as they realize that the Tidal Heart has willingly stilled its vibrant energy, signaling its readiness to be freed from its prison within the cave. With a sense of purpose and determination, they prepare to transport it safely to its rightful throne, where its energy can be re-energized and its powers restored. They recognize the significance of this task and the responsibility that comes with it, knowing that the fate of their world may very well depend on the successful completion of their mission. With hearts full of hope and resolve, they set out to fulfill their duty, guided by the ancient wisdom whispered within the depths of the Tidal Heart.

Marina and Dolphinea move with synchronized grace as they take turns cradling the Tidal Heart in the center of their flukes, securing it snugly between the tips of their tail fins. They navigate the narrow cave passageways with gentle precision, relying on their keen echolocation abilities to guide them through the darkness. Each movement is deliberate, each turn calculated, as they carry their precious cargo with the utmost care. As they emerge from the cave's confines into the open waters of the shelf, a sense of relief washes over them. Waiting to assist them are Sol and Varden, their loyal companions, ready to lend a helping hand as the foursome brings the Tidal Heart to the surface. With synchronized effort, the foursome carefully guided the Tidal Heart into the shallow waters next to the Blue Horizon.

In its present form, the Tidal Heart manifests as an aqua blue sphere, possessing a size roughly equivalent to two large turtle shells, with the outer shell facing outwards in either direction. Its surface gleams with mesmerizing aqua-blue transparency, hinting at the ancient power contained within its depths. When fully activated, its size increases as its properties transform into an iridescent sphere of pulsating power and color. As it rests in the shallow waters beside the Blue Horizon, its presence commands attention, radiating an aura of mystique and significance that captivates all who behold it. Though seemingly unassuming in appearance, the Tidal Heart holds the potential to shape the destiny of the ocean tides and currents, serving as a beacon of hope in a world fraught with uncertainty.

Captain Dan enters the water, his gaze fixed on the task at hand. Meanwhile, Milo, his trusted first mate, swings a makeshift crane and boom over the port side of the Blue Horizon, carefully lowering an oversized chest into the water below. As the chest splashes down, Varden, Dolphinea, and Marina spring into action, maneuvering the

Tidal Heart with precision and skill. Resting on Varden's hard shell back, just at the surface's waterline. The Tidal Heart glimmers enchantingly in the sunlight as Captain Dan deftly maneuvers it into the open chest, its radiant hues dancing in the gentle ocean breeze. With a sense of reverence, Captain Dan closes the lid of the chest, sealing the ancient artifact within its protective confines. He then signals to Milo, who swiftly operates the crane and boom, lifting the chest with the Tidal Heart securely nestled inside. With practiced precision, Milo carefully deposits the chest onto the deck of the Blue Horizon, ensuring that the precious cargo remains safe, secure, and undisturbed for the journey ahead.

As the alliance members look on, a sense of accomplishment fills the air, marking the successful completion of this crucial part of their mission. The team gathers at the stern platform with the Tidal Heart safely stored aboard the Blue Horizon. Kaia tells them that Jasper will need at least the remainder of the day before he is recovered enough to travel. Captain Dan informs them that he and Milo have spotted a fishing vessel anchored about two miles east of them, just inside the shallow waters of the shelf off Soldiers Cay. He relays his suspicions that they have been observing the alliance's activities this morning, and he feels uncomfortable about their presence in such proximity.

The group is concerned and alarmed at the prospect of facing the unknown fisherman and their vessel, especially not knowing their intentions. Captain Dan suggests that the Blue Horizon and the alliance members depart in the darkness of night, silently sailing south-southeast, avoiding the fishing vessel and its crew's prying, scanning eyes. "We can correct our heading once we are clear of the shelf and have distanced ourselves from the fishing vessel," he adds. "Meanwhile," he continues, "we will keep our distance but keep our eyes on them for any movement or signals of danger. Nereus will patrol the eastern waters; his sleekness and speed will be an asset, preventing him from being detected. "

The members express their agreement with the plan through quiet clicks, chirps, gestures, and low guttural sounds. Dolphinea translates for the group. The rest of the day, Captain Dan and Milo prepare the Blue Horizon for the next leg of their voyage. Fuel is low in the tanks, so they check the wind direction, weather forecast, and charts. Knowing they must rely heavily on the wind and their sails, they check the rigging, canvas, mast, and beams for seaworthiness. Dolphinea, Marina, and Sol gather schools of fish for them and the others to dine on. They relax in the shallows, taking turns cat-napping while semi-consciously alert as they wait for nightfall. Kaia and Varden dine and relax closer to the shore, where the seagrass and seaweed are most abundant and provide the most protection. Jasper remains with them, recovering from his wounds.

As darkness descends upon Ambergris Cay and its neighboring waters, the crew of the Blue Horizon dims the cabin lights and prepares to set sail. With practiced hands, they unfurl the sails, taking advantage of the wind from the north-northwest. These favorable conditions allow them to sail downwind in a south-southeasterly direction, keeping the sails open to catch the wind from behind. The mainsail acts as a foil, working in tandem with the spinnaker to harness the full force of the breeze and propel the Blue Horizon forward with grace and speed. As the night envelops them and the stars twinkle overhead, Captain Dan steers their vessel confidently into the darkness, guided by the gentle whisper of the wind.

Dolphinea and Marina glide effortlessly along the port side of the sailing ship, their sleek forms slicing through the water with precision and grace. On the starboard side, Jasper and Sol maintain a vigilant watch as they glide along, their keen eyes scanning the horizon for any signs of danger. Kaia and Varden trail behind the stern of the boat, their large flippers propelling them through the water with ease as they effortlessly keep pace with the vessel.

Meanwhile, Nereus leads the way, threading through the water significantly ahead of the ship and the rest of the alliance members. With silent determination, the group moves as one, their movements coordinated and synchronized as they silently slip past the eyes of the crew on the fishing vessel anchored across the aquatic shelf. In the cover of darkness, they remain unseen, their mission shrouded in secrecy as they continue their journey toward their ultimate destination.

Midway through the night, Milo, the vigilant lookout on the Blue Horizon, notices a blip on the surface radar screen, indicating a vessel approximately five miles behind them. With caution, Milo alerts Captain Dan, who emerges onto the deck to assess the situation. Under the canopy of a starlit sky and the waning moon, Captain Dan squints into the darkness, discerning the silhouette of the pursuing vessel growing steadily closer.

A sense of unease settles over Captain Dan and Milo as they realize they are being followed in the dead of night. Tension mounts as Captain Dan and his first mate brace themselves for the impending encounter. With every passing moment, the distant hum of engines grows louder, signaling the imminent arrival of the mysterious vessel. As the vessel draws nearer, Captain Dan recognizes it as the same fishing vessel stalking them at Ambergris Cay. Captain Dan jumps into action, deepening the sail draft by easing the main sheet, giving the Blue Horizon a burst of speed. As the Blue Horizon picks up momentum, Captain Dan's strategic maneuver allows them to widen the gap between their vessel and the pursuer behind them.

With each passing moment, the distant silhouette of the pursuing vessel grows smaller on the horizon, gradually falling behind as the Blue Horizon gains distance and leaves its potential threat in its wake. Captain Dan's quick thinking and decisive action gave them the advantage they needed to outmaneuver their pursuer and ensure the safety of the members of the alliance and their precious cargo. Maintaining a steady pace and a true bearing southeast, the marine armada of humans and ocean companions, with sails billowing on the Blue Horizon, is pushed forward by a strong wind and a swift current through the night.

As the morning light spills across the waters of the Bahamas, painting the sky in hues of pastel pink and gold, a sense of tranquility descends upon the scene. The Blue Horizon glides smoothly through the strait, separating Nassau from Eleuthera's northern tip. In the distance, the towering peaks of Eleuthera rise majestically against the horizon, their verdant slopes bathed in the soft light of dawn.

Further ahead of them, two magnificent humpback whales breach the surface with raw power and elegance. Their massive bodies arch gracefully against the azure sky, sending cascades of shimmering droplets into the air. As the whales catch sight of the approaching Blue Horizon and its alliance, they change course and draw nearer. With each powerful stroke of their tails, they propel themselves through the water, closing the distance between themselves and the vessel with astonishing speed. As the whales gracefully join the procession of dolphins and turtles, their presence brings a sense of ancient wisdom and a profound connection to the ocean's depths. With silent communication that transcends language, Dolphinea and the whales form a bond of understanding and purpose. There's a shared recognition of the importance of their quest and the significance of the Tidal Heart, an artifact of immense power.

Dolphinea and the whales exchange a knowing glance, acknowledging the sacredness of their mission and each alliance member's role in its fulfillment. The whales reveal their knowledge of the ancient ruins hidden beneath the waves and the precise location of the throne, where the Tidal Heart awaits its rightful place.

With gratitude and reverence, Dolphinea accepts the whales' offer to guide the alliance to their destination. With the combined strength, wisdom, and unity of the creatures of the sea, they set forth on their journey, their hearts filled with determination and hope as they ventured toward the fulfillment of their quest and the restoration of balance to the underwater realm.

# ❧ CHAPTER SIXTEEN ❧

On the Blue Horizon, Captain Dan knows they are running short on food, supplies, fuel, and necessities; however, he decides to press on rather than make port and draw attention. After their mission is accomplished, there will be plenty of time to replenish the ship's stores. Noticing that the two whales have joined the alliance and seem to be taking up a lead position, Captain Dan alters course to follow their lead as the other members synchronize with the two humpback's movements, as the armada presses on.

Passing the island of Nassau aboard the Blue Horizon. Milo's mind drifts back to the carefree days of his youth spent wandering the island's vibrant streets and sandy shores. Nassau and Paradise Island hold a special place as the gateway to the Bahamas, where turquoise waters meet powdery beaches and colorful culture. Memories of the bustling Straw Market, the majestic resorts, and the rhythmic beats of Junkanoo dances flood Milo's thoughts, transporting him back to a time of innocence and wonder amidst the tropical paradise.

The morning sun dances on the waters as Dolphinea and Marina swim side by side. Nearing the completion of their quest and mission to return the Title Heart to its home among the ancient ruins hidden in the waters of the Bahamas, they reflect on their journey together and reminisce about home and the precious moments they shared there with each other. They miss their families. and long for the halcyon days that they once enjoyed. As they glide gracefully through the crystal-clear waters, memories flood their minds: laughter echoing through their homes, the warmth of familial embraces, and the simple joys of everyday life. Dolphinea and Marina exchange fond glances, silently acknowledging the bond that has grown between them during their adventurous journey.

Together, they have faced challenges and overcome obstacles, relying on each other for strength and support. And though they may be far from home, they carry with them the love and memories that sustain them through their journey. They know that no matter how far they roam, home will always be waiting for them. Love gleams in Marina's eyes as they swim together. Their hearts beat as one, and their breaths, in rhythmic cadence, mingled with the salty breeze and the gentle lapping of the waves against their skin.

The waters surrounding Nassau and Eleuthera in the Bahamas are a picturesque haven for fishing boats, leisure craft, and visitors alike, teeming with diverse marine life. Serving as the capital of the Bahamas, Nassau is not only a bustling hub for governance but also a significant port in the Caribbean region. Its allure as one of the world's premier pleasure resorts draws tourists from across the globe, eager to experience its vibrant culture and stunning natural landscapes. The waters here offer recreational opportunities and a glimpse into the rich biodiversity of the Caribbean Sea, with marine creatures ranging from colorful tropical fish to majestic dolphins.

Nassau's natural beauty extends beyond its azure waters, with offshore marine gardens dotting the eastern end of the harbor, showcasing the region's vibrant underwater ecosystems. On land, the landscape is adorned with lush vegetation, including scarlet poinciana trees, vibrant poinsettias, and cascading purple bougainvillea, adding splashes of color to the island's picturesque vistas. Additionally, Paradise Island, linked to Nassau by two bridges, stands as a luxurious tourist haven, boasting high-rise hotels and glamorous casinos. This paradise complements Nassau's offerings and serves as a protective barrier, sheltering the city's excellent natural harbor and accommodating cruise ships of all sizes, further enhancing the area's allure as a premier destination in the Caribbean.

Navigating through the waters between Nassau and Bar Bay, Eleuthera, Captain Dan sails the Blue Horizon straight through the center of the two islands, approximately fifteen miles offshore. This gives the alliance some degree of anonymity and separation, away from curious fishermen and tourist vessels. As the gap between Nassau and Eleuthera widens, the open waters offer the marine companions the perfect opportunity for leisure swimming. Dolphinea and his dolphin companions Marina, Jasper, and Sol gracefully leap in and out of the waves; their playful antics restore the friendships and bonds they have for each other as they arc through the water with effortless grace. Varden and Kaia, the two wise and noble green turtles, glide serenely beneath the surface, their movements unhurried and tranquil, lending an air of calm to the vibrant seascape. Meanwhile, Nereus, the swift and bold swordfish, darts and dives, his sleek body slicing through the water with astonishing speed and agility, his occasional leaps adding a thrilling spectacle to the maritime panorama.

Amidst this aquatic symphony, the two majestic humpback whales emerge from the depths, their massive forms breaching the surface with breathtaking power. With each breach, they send plumes of water cascading into the air before gracefully submerging again, their synchronized swimming a testament to the harmony of the ocean's depths. As they dive, their massive bodies create ripples that reverberate across the expanse, a reminder of the awe-inspiring beauty and majesty beneath the surface of the Bahamian waters. Together, these marine companions paint a vivid portrait of life in the open seas, where every movement celebrates the boundless wonders that abound in this pristine aquatic realm.

The frenzied activity of the dolphins, turtles, swordfish, and whales in the open waters creates a captivating spectacle that draws curious schools of fish to the surface, creating a veritable dining smorgasbord. As the commotion and turbulence churn the water, the scent of abundance attracts opportunistic seagulls and seabirds overhead. The birds dive from above with precision and agility, plunging into the water to snatch fish above and below the surface. Their shrill cries mingle with their marine companions' splashing and playful chatter, forming a vibrant symphony. As the commotion gradually subsides, a sense of tranquility settles over the seas again, restoring a serene balance to the maritime realm. The members of the alliance resume their journey. gracefully navigating the waters with a sense of ease and satisfaction.

Deep within the annals of Lucayan legend lies the tale of an ancient ocean civilization that once ruled the seas and currents surrounding the Bahamas. According to the lore passed down through generations, this enigmatic civilization possessed a profound understanding of the intricate rhythms and flows of the ocean, harnessing its power with remarkable precision. Legends speak of colossal vessels that traversed the waters effortlessly, guided by the wisdom of their seafaring ancestors. However, their island domain, a majestic paradise that thrived in harmony with the marine realm, met its tragic fate during a cataclysmic upheaval of the earth, plunging beneath the waves in a moment of unfathomable destruction.

Yet a tale of resilience and survival rose from the ashes of this ancient civilization. The survivors, guided by the memory of their lost homeland and the legacy of their ancestors, dispersed across the scattered islands of the Bahamas, seeking refuge amidst the turquoise waters and sun-kissed shores. They carried with them the remnants of their once-great civilization, preserving the knowledge and traditions of their forebears amidst the trials of their new existence.

Over time, the ancient ruins and artifacts, many of them lost to the depths and left behind by their vanished civilization, became sacred relics, serving as a poignant reminder of a lost era and a testament to the enduring spirit of the Lucayan people. One of those relics lost to the sea had the power to control the ocean's tides and currents; that relic was known as the Tidal Heart. And so, the survivors forged a new chapter in their history, weaving their legacy into the fabric of the Bahamian islands, where the echoes of their ancestors continue to resonate through the currents of time.

Just before noon, the Blue Horizon and its alliance of human and marine members arrived in the waters northwest of Powell Point in the Eleutheras. Captain Dan and Milo lowered the sails and dropped anchor at a depth of fifty feet, two miles off the tip of Powell Point. Captain Dan checked the underwater terrain with the onboard instruments and pinged a reading on the array indicating underwater structures at an approximate depth of seven hundred and fifty feet just west of their location. Communicating with Dolphinea at the stern platform, Captain Dan relayed his findings to his dolphin companion, who translated this information to the aquatic members of the alliance. The two humpback whale members, Eurus (the male) and Ula (the female), confirm that the reading is accurate based on their knowledge and the legends passed down through their generations.

Captain Dan puts on his scuba gear and enters the water as Milo fastens the chest to the end of the boom with rope and chain, swinging the crane and boom over the water and lowering the chest into Captain Dan's waiting arms. The captain opened the chest and cradled the soft pastel aqua blue sphere within his arms, feeling its subtle pulsating heart for the first time. The Tidal Heart, glowing with an otherworldly luminescence, seems to radiate an aura of tranquility that envelops Captain Dan. With each gentle pulse, he feels a connection to timeless wisdom, a profound understanding that transcends the boundaries of the present moment. The sensation is akin to being submerged in a sea of sensation and knowledge, where the currents of ancient wisdom flow effortlessly around him, whispering secrets of the past and insights into the future. In this sacred moment, Captain Dan is at one with the sphere, his senses attuned to its subtle energies and vibrations—a moment he will remember for the rest of his days.

Captain Dan transfers the Tidal Heart to Dolphinea and Marina as they cradle it between themselves, their pectoral fins overlapping, their torsos touching as they swim side by side, their flukes for propulsion, and their remaining outer pectoral fins for steering. Following in close proximity and in the wake left by Eurus and Ula, Dolphinea. Marina, Sol, and Jasper begin their descent to the deeper waters where the ancient ruins lay. Varden and Kaia, also guided by Eurus and Ula, fall into the rear of the procession. Captain Dan returns to the Blue Horizon, and he and Milo store the crane, boom, chest, and equipment.

Descending into the ocean's depths, the light above grew dimmer, replaced by the eerie glow of bio-luminescent creatures inhabiting the abyssal zone. Their descent was steady and controlled. The water around them was cold and silent. Approaching the ocean floor, the silhouette of the ancient ruins began to take shape, looming like silent guardians of a forgotten era. Massive stone structures rose from the seabed, their weathered surfaces adorned with intricate carvings and faded symbols. Crumbled statues stood sentinel, their once-majestic forms now eroded by centuries beneath the waves. Columns stretched towards the surface, remnants of grand temples and meeting places now submerged in the watery abyss. Schools of fish darted among the ruins, their movements adding a sense of life to the otherwise still landscape.

As they ventured deeper into the heart of the ruins, the companions marveled at the intricate details that adorned every surface. Ancient tablets lined crumbled walls, their inscriptions hinting at the wisdom and knowledge of a civilization long gone. Cracked statues depicting gods and goddesses, their features worn by time but still retaining an air of majesty and power. Columns soared overhead, their once-polished surfaces now covered in a patina of algae and coral, yet still standing as a testament to the craftsmanship of their creators. Amidst the ruins, remnants of temples and meeting places lay scattered, their foundations offering glimpses into the daily lives and rituals of the ancient inhabitants.

Eurus and Ula break off their lead just above a temple's ruins. Gazing back at Dolphinea and the group, they nod, indicating they have reached their destination. As Dolphinea, Marina, and their companions reach the temple, they see an open chamber, its roof long gone from ages of erosion, exposing the interior to the sea above, and realize this is the heart of the ancient ruins. They are met with a breathtaking sight—a majestic throne, intricately carved from stone, stands at the center of the chamber. Surrounding the throne are ornate pillars adorned with symbols of the ocean's power, and there are faces of ancient guardians carved into the walls, watching the open chamber with silent reverence. With a sense of awe, they realize this is the rightful place for the Tidal Heart—the seat of power for the ocean's currents.

With solemn determination, Dolphinea and Marina carefully place the Tidal Heart upon the throne, its pulsating energy resonating with the ancient stones. As they back away from the throne, anticipation fills the open chamber, as if the air is holding its breath in anticipation of what will come. Suddenly, a radiant glow envelops the throne, illuminating the chamber with a dazzling display of light and color. The Tidal Heart, at the center of its sanctuary, begins to pulse with an otherworldly energy that spreads outward, touching every corner of the ocean in and around the ruins.

A surge of immense energy erupts from the artifact, and brilliant hues of blue and green spring forth from its core, illuminating the chamber with a dazzling display of color. The once-muted ruins are bathed in the radiant glow, and phosphorescent orbs dance around the chamber, weaving intricate patterns in the air. Caught off guard by the sudden burst of energy, Dolphinea and his companions are propelled backward, their bodies twisting and turning in a whirlwind of motion. Head over tails, they somersault through the water, caught in the mesmerizing spectacle unfolding before them.

Despite the chaotic momentum, a sense of awe and wonder fills their hearts as they witness the raw power of the Tidal Heart in action. As the energy surge subsides, the chamber is bathed in a serene glow, and the dolphins find themselves floating amidst the remnants of the dazzling display. With each breath, they feel the renewed strength of the ocean currents coursing through their bodies. With reverence, Dolphinea, Marina, and their companions gaze upon the artifact, knowing their journey has led to this triumph. The ocean's seabed begins to rumble, and the waters begin to churn.

The dolphin and turtle alliance members begin their ascent from the ancient ruins towards the surface. They struggled against the currents the quaking ocean floor created, dragging them down; panic threatened to overwhelm them. Just as their air and hope dwindled, Eurus and Ula answered their silent plea for assistance. Emerging from the fathomless depths, the majestic whales positioned themselves above and in front of the group, their powerful forms creating a protective barrier against the raging waters. With a graceful sweep of their ethereal tails, Eurus and Ula conjured a swirling vortex, a mesmerizing aquatic funnel that drew the beleaguered members toward the surface.

With each passing moment, the pressure of the depths began to ease, replaced by a sense of weightlessness as they ascended towards the welcoming embrace of the surface. As they breached the ocean's surface, gasping for air, they bathed in the warm glow of sunlight, their rescuers Eurus and Ula watching over them with benevolent eyes. Grateful and awestruck, the group offered silent thanks to these giant guardians, whose intervention had saved them from a watery grave.

As Captain Dan gazed out from the deck of the Blue Horizon, he beheld a spectacle unlike any other. The seas glowed in a brilliant display of illuminations of blues and greens radiating into the sky above him. The waters churned, and waves swelled around the anchored sailboat, tossing it to and fro and putting immense strain on the anchor chain and hull. Phosphorescent orbs rose out of the water and danced around the Blue Horizon. The orbs pulsed and undulated, casting an otherworldly light on the water that seemed to defy explanation. It was as if the very fabric of space had come alive, weaving a mesmerizing tapestry of light and shadow. As Captain Dan stood in awe, he felt a sense of reverence wash over him. It was as if he had been granted a glimpse into the secrets of the universe, a fleeting moment of connection with something far greater than himself.

# ❧ CHAPTER SEVENTEEN ❧

From the shores of Eleuthera to Nassau, Paradise Island, and throughout the Bahamas, the inhabitants beheld the spectacle of glimmering lights in the sky and on the waters, turbulent seas, and the power of the Tidal Heart. Not understanding what was happening around them, the inhabitants feared the worst at first, but as the chaotic waters began to calm and stabilize, a sense of peace and harmony filled their hearts. Under the waves, with a dazzling display of light and sound, the currents of the Atlantic Ocean begin to shift and swirl, restoring balance and harmony to the underwater world.

With the Tidal Heart protected by the depths and its fused connection to the ancient throne, the ancient guardian of the tides and currents, pulsating with renewed energy, its mystical influence extends far beyond the confines of the ancient ruins. In the vast expanse of the North Atlantic, the once-dormant underwater streams awaken with newfound vigor. The mighty Gulf Stream currents, which had faltered in their course, now surge forth with unparalleled strength and purpose. With each powerful surge, warmer waters from the south are propelled northward, breaking through the barriers of cold and stagnation that had gripped the northern seas.

As the Gulf Stream currents flow as they were meant to, a remarkable transformation unfolds across the North Atlantic. The colder waters of the north, which had been starved of essential nutrients and warmth, are now invigorated by the influx of warmer currents. The ebb and flow of tides in the south regain their natural rhythm, creating a harmonious balance that reverberates throughout the underwater world. Dolphinea, Marina, and their companions witness this awe-inspiring spectacle with joy and gratitude, knowing that their quest to restore the Tidal Heart has brought about a profound change that will benefit marine life for generations.

As the sun descends towards the horizon, painting the waters of Eleuthera with soft hues of color, the tranquil scene is accentuated by the backdrop of clear blue skies and puffs of white clouds. A gentle breeze originating from the southeast whispers through the air, creating a soothing rhythm that harmonizes with the calmness of the seas. Weighing anchor Captain Dan brings the Blue Horizon into port at Powell Point by inboard motor, using the remaining fuel in the vessel's tanks. Radioing ahead ship to shore, he reserves a slip at Seaside Resort and Marina.

Varden and Kaia, the two noble green turtles of the alliance, settle in for the night along the grassy shoreline and protected inlet south of Powell Point. Dolphinea, Marina, Jasper, and Sol decide the inlet would be ideal for them to dine and retire for the night. Exhausted from the long voyage and the day's activities, culminating in the successful completion of their quest, the dolphins and turtles fall asleep, with the gentle sounds of inlet waters lapping against the shoreline and the distant sounds of music and celebration from the resort and marina to the north.

As the sun dipped below the horizon and the night spread across the sky, the atmosphere at Seaside Resort and Marina became charged with a palpable sense of joy and relief. Tourists, visitors, and residents mingled; their faces lit up with smiles as they recounted the breathtaking spectacle they had witnessed. The sea, once turbulent and chaotic, now seemed tranquil.

Amidst the music and laughter, Captain Dan and Milo found themselves seated at a table overlooking the shimmering waters of the Bahamas. With an immense sense of profound accomplishment washing over them, they raised their glasses in a toast, acknowledging not only their efforts but also the efforts of their ocean companions. "To us," Captain Dan said, his voice filled with pride, "for braving the unknown and helping to restore balance to the ocean's depths." "And to Dolphinea and the alliance!" he added. "Yes to our companions and to the Tidal Heart," Milo said, his eyes sparkling with admiration, "for guiding us and showing us the way."

Their glasses clinked together, the sound echoing in the warm evening air. Around them, others joined in the toast, their voices blending into a chorus of celebration. As they savored the moment, Captain Dan and Milo couldn't help but feel a sense of awe at what they had witnessed, experienced, and accomplished during their most remarkable journey. They knew they had been a part of something truly magical and essential, something wondrous and extraordinary that would be remembered for generations.

The morning greeted the shores of Eleuthera and the waters of the Bahamas with unparalleled splendor, marking the arrival of a day unlike any other. Its vibrancy, brilliance, and magnificence painted a breathtaking picture that seemed almost surreal. In the embrace of this dawn, schools of fish thrived abundantly, their movements a mesmerizing dance beneath the surface, while above, sea birds and seagulls soared gracefully, adding to the spectacle with their elegant flight patterns. The waters themselves were a stunning mosaic, blending hues of blues, pastels, and aqua greens to display nature's artistry.

A gentle sea breeze wafted from the southeast, carrying a whisper of the ocean's secrets. Meanwhile, the water currents flowed steadily from the east, their rhythmic motion enveloping the islands in a tender embrace. In this dance of gentle grace, the currents delivered much-needed nutrients to the coral beds and underwater marine environment, nurturing life in every crevice and corner of the sea. It was a harmonious symphony of nature, where every element played its part in sustaining the ecosystem's delicate balance.

Dolphinea, Marina, their dolphin, and turtle companions swam the short distance to the Seaside Resort and Marina within the small harbor entrance at Powell Point. Locating the slip where the Blue Dolphin moored, they gathered at the stern platform of the vessel. Captain Dan and Milo were already awake and onboard, replenishing supplies and stowing away gear. Seeing Dolphinea and the others gathered, Captain Dan stopped what he was doing and excitedly dropped to one knee at the stern platform, reaching a hand down to greet his ocean companions. The connection was immediate and reciprocal as Dolphinea raised his bottled nose in a gentle nudge against Captain Dan's outstretched hand. Then Dolphinea braised his side against the captain's hand. Marina, Jasper, and Sol followed the same actions to show appreciation and affection.

Tears welled up in Captain Dan's eyes as he was overwhelmed by the closeness and affection his special dolphin companions greeted him with. Knowing they would soon part, there was still a sense of togetherness and friendship between them that would last a lifetime. In their special telepathic language, Dolphinea began, his thoughts reaching out to Captain Dan. "Today, Marina, Jasper, Sol, and I will depart for our home waters. But before we depart, I want to express our deepest gratitude to you and Milo. Your unwavering companionship and assistance throughout our quest to restore the Tidal Heart to its rightful place have been invaluable," he paused, his gratitude overflowing. "Without your guidance, we could never have achieved our goal of restoring the tides and currents to their natural balance."

Dolphinea's thoughts continued, his bond with Captain Dan, which was evident: "You have been more than just a captain to us; you have been a trusted friend and confidant. You will always be welcomed in our home waters, and your friendship will forever hold a special place in our hearts." He concluded with sincerity, "I am forever indebted to you for your service and your friendship, my captain, my friend."

With heartfelt sincerity, Captain Dan responded to Dolphinea, his words conveyed with deep emotion: "My dear Dolphinea, you hold a special place in my heart, no matter where the winds and waves may carry me. Your unwavering courage and determination have been an inspiration to me throughout our journey." He paused briefly, reflecting on their shared experiences, before continuing, "Thank you for allowing me the privilege of being a part of this noble quest, for it has been an honor to stand by your side."

Captain Dan's voice softened as he spoke of Dolphinea's uncle: "Please convey my heartfelt regards to your Uncle Jinn and express my gratitude for guiding you to me. Like him, you have become my cherished companion of the ocean, and I am forever indebted to you for the wisdom and gifts you have bestowed upon me." He concluded with genuine warmth, "You will always be my hero, my dear Dolphinea, and in my heart, you are my family."

The four dolphin companions, Dolphinea, Marina, Jasper, and Sol, turned on their sides and, with a wave of their pectoral fins, departed the stern of the Blue Horizon and the marina at Powell Point. The two green turtles, Varden and Kaia, also bid their farewells, extending their large arm-like pectoral fins in a wave of gratitude and admiration to Captain Dan, Milo, and their four dolphin companions, and also departed the marina. Varden and Kaia decided to remain in the waters and sea grasses surrounding Eleuthera, knowing that the balance in the oceans and the restoration of the currents would bring an abundance of nutrients, seaweed, and kelp from the Sargasso Sea to the Bahamas.

Reaching the open waters, Dolphinea and his three companions spotted Eurus and Ula breaching in the distance as the two humpback whales waved a farewell and a wish for swift currents to the four dolphins as they embarked on their journey home. Nereus is spotted swiftly gliding through the open water, diving and jumping out of the water, and performing spins before splashing back to the surface. With clicks and a chorus of whistles, they acknowledge this magnificent fish's contribution to the alliance and will always be grateful to him.

With a speedy current from the southeast and the trade winds at their backs, the dolphin's journey home would take them northwest towards Nassau and then past the northern tip of the main island of Bahama before reaching the familiar waters of Coral Cove and Lumina Island. If the winds and swift currents prevail, they should get home in about two days following this route. With their unmatched speed and agility, the four dolphins surged toward home, effortlessly harnessing the swift currents to propel them onward. Darting through the crystal-clear waters gracefully and precisely, they covered the distance to Nassau in record time, their journey spanning less than a single day.

Stopping only to gather a school of herring for a late afternoon meal and a brief rest period, the four friends continue their journey as evening approaches. Freed from time and space constraints, they surged ahead into the night, their determination unwavering. As they swam, the dolphins noticed a distinct change in the ocean water around them. It felt purer, fresher, with a reduced saltiness, yet enriched with nutrients and healing properties that invigorated their senses. Each breath of air seemed to carry a newfound cleanliness and sweetness, heightening their experience of the world around them. Above, the night sky unfolded in a breathtaking display, alive with sparkling stars and vibrant ribbons of stellar constellations stretching as far as the eye could see. At this moment, amidst the vast ocean and sky, the dolphins felt a profound connection to the natural beauty and wonder of the universe.

As the first signs of daybreak emerged, Dolphinea, Marina, Jasper, and Sol rounded the northern tip of Bahama Island. In the soft light of dawn, they were greeted by a breathtaking sight: flocks of pink flamingos, now native to the Bahamas, adorned the shores at Red Bay, their vibrant plumage casting a vivid contrast against the golden hues of the morning sky. Stretching across the entire tip of the island, the flamingos created a stunning tableau of natural beauty, symbolizing the harmony and resilience of the island's ecosystem.

Coral Cove and Lumina Island buzzed with excitement and anticipation as the morning sun cast its warm glow from the east. News spread quickly through the dolphin communities, carried by aerial messengers. The four dolphin explorers had successfully rounded the northern tip of Bahama Island and were coming home, expecting to arrive later in the day. The anticipation was palpable as both pods prepared to welcome back their beloved friends and family members, their hearts filled with joy and relief at the prospect of their safe return. Celebration electrified the air as the elders from both pods, united in anticipation, decreed that Dolphinea and Sol's pod members would converge with those of Marina and Jasper's pod at Coral Cove for a grand welcome home celebration. Two days prior, the elders had sensed a shift in the ocean currents and the whispers of the winds, signaling the success of the dolphins' noble quest. The seas and skies bore witness to a remarkable transformation, with tides and currents returning to a harmonious balance and the once-thriving sea life and flora flourishing once more in abundance. Moreover, the looming threat of predators had dissipated, leaving the azure blue waters across the Bahamas and the Caribbean teeming with newfound tranquility and security.

As the sun ascended over Coral Cove and Lumina Island, preparations for the festivities were in full swing. The atmosphere hummed with anticipation, excitement, and joy as pods from both communities gathered, eager to welcome back their valiant friends. With hearts overflowing with gratitude and pride, the elders looked on, knowing that this day marked the triumphant return of the dolphins and the restoration of balance and harmony to the waters they called home.

Swimming together, Dolphinea and Marina conversed about the exceptional journey and adventure they and the others had experienced, relishing the memories of overcoming challenges and forging new bonds. As they glided effortlessly through the crystal-clear waters, they discussed how the future had been secured for themselves, their families, and the pod members. With each stroke, excitement and joy filled their hearts as they anticipated returning home, now just half a day away, where they could enjoy well-deserved leisure time together.

Swimming nearby, Jasper and Sol shared the excitement of returning to their families and male alliances. Their jovial banter echoed in the ocean depths as they chuckled through loud whistles and clicks, splashing their tails up and down in exuberance. The prospect of reuniting with loved ones and resuming their roles in the pod filled them with joy, their playful antics serving as a testament to the strong bonds they shared and their community.

The air buzzed with excitement as the dolphins' return drew near. With its vibrant marine life and shimmering waters, Coral Cove was a scene of anticipation and celebration. The two dolphin pods, united in their support for their heroes, made final preparations, ensuring everything was just right for the awaited arrival. Schools of fish darted through the water, herded earlier in preparation for the feast. Families of the four adventurous dolphins moved nervously yet joyously, eagerly awaiting the moment they would be reunited with their loved ones.

Amidst the bustling activity, the elders took center stage, sharing wisdom and tales of ancient legends and dolphin lore. Their words resonated through the crowd, passing down traditions and stories to the next generation. As the sun reached its zenith, the festivities reached a crescendo, with laughter and joy echoing through the cove. Each community member played their part, contributing to the energy and excitement that filled the air. At long last, as the sun reached noon, the anticipation peaked. All eyes were on the horizon, eagerly scanning for the first signs of the returning heroes. Hearts raced with anticipation, and cheers erupted as the familiar shapes of the dolphins appeared in the distance. The moment of reunion was at hand, marking the culmination of weeks of preparation and anticipation.

As Dolphinea, Marina, Jasper, and Sol approached the waters of Coral Cove, they could see a frenzy in the water ahead of them. As they got closer, they could make out their friends' and families' familiar silhouettes and faces. Excitement came over the four weary but joyous travelers. Emotions ran high as the dolphins gracefully returned to the embrace of their families and fellow pod members, greeted by cheers, applause, and the warm embrace of their loved ones. Everyone was there. Marina's mother, Maris, embraced her, whispering, "Now, my daughter, you have accomplished great things," as her siblings pranced in the water around them. Jasper's proud parents and siblings were greeting him with nudges and affection, and Sol's family was there to honor their brave and courageous son. The homecoming celebration was like no other one that anyone could ever remember.

Dolphinea's mother, Luna, and his father, Delphin, embraced their son as their hearts swelled with pride and exaltation. "I am so very proud of you, my son. I love you with all my heart," she said to him as she gazed at him with loving eyes. His father, Delphin, gave him a knowing wink and extended his pectoral fin to his son, which Dolphinea, with great respect and reverence, accepted. Uncle Jinn said with a smile, "You must tell me all about your most exceptional adventure, my nephew."

The sun bathed Coral Cove in its golden light, and the celebrations continued long into the afternoon and evening. The journey of the four adventurous dolphins had come full circle, returning them home to their pod's embrace and their families' loving arms.

As night falls and the ocean grows still, Dolphinea drifts into a peaceful slumber. In his dreams, echoes of his underwater adventures come to life, magnified and embellished by his imagination. With Marina by his side, he embarks on even grander quests, encountering mythical sea creatures, magical artifacts, seafarers, and ocean allies, and unraveling ancient mysteries hidden beneath the waves.

When morning breaks and the soft light filters through the water, Dolphinea awakens with a start. The memories of his dream adventures linger, leaving him disoriented. Was it all just a figment of his imagination? But then, a familiar voice echoes through the water. It is the voice of Marina, his mate and closest companion, who had journeyed alongside him through every twist and turn of their underwater odyssey. With a gentle nudge, she swims closer to Dolphinea and whispers these simple yet profound words: "It's good to be home."

At that moment, Dolphinea's heart swells with warmth and relief. The line between dream and reality blurs, leaving him to wonder if the adventures he experienced were merely the products of his imagination or if they genuinely unfolded beneath the waves.

Feeling a sense of contentment settle over him, Dolphinea reached out to Marina, wrapping her in a loving embrace. With its familiar sights and comforting presence, home suddenly felt like the most wondrous place in the world. In that moment, he realizes that perhaps the greatest adventures are the ones shared with loved ones right in the comfort of home.

Finis

www.ingramcontent.com/pod-product-compliance
Lightning Source LLC
Chambersburg PA
CBHW020317260626
47156CB00004B/1258